Lisbon Tales

Stories translated by
Amanda Hopkinson

Edited by
Helen Constantine

OXFORD
UNIVERSITY PRESS

I would like to thank Victor Meadowcroft for his contribution to this translation. A native Lisboan, he was both an excellent guide and fellow traveller through many chapters of its literary history.

Contents

Picture Credits

General Introduction

Those who are fascinated by the history of a city will find that Lisbon will not disappoint. Be it the ancient Alfama district, a survival from the capture by the Moors in the eighth century, with its medieval castle; the Torre de Belém in the harbour, the monument to the voyages of discovery in the fifteenth, sixteenth, and seventeenth centuries; or the Carmo Convent commemorating the catastrophic Lisbon earthquake of 1755; there is much to be admired or pondered in a visit to this, generally considered the most ancient, city in Europe. From the Greek and Phoenician traders, to invasions by the Romans and Moors, to Napoleon, the Second World War, and its subsequent regimes, Lisbon, with its many layers of culture and influence will reveal to the attentive visitor its triumphs and its wounds.

Every city has its unique character, yet, paradoxically, everyone's experience of that city will be different. We all choose to visit different sights, we meet different people, and so on. My own visit, far too brief, was nonetheless an unforgettable feast for the senses. Apart from the soft sounds of the Portuguese language still whispering in my head, I carried home abiding memories of houses covered in flowers and many-coloured tiles; of little boys clinging onto wooden trams to hitch a ride up the very steep streets; of the sharpness of fresh sardines; of the bronze statue of Pessoa on the crowded square; and especially of Fado, those melancholy songs and their singers that stay with you long after you leave and seem to express the very essence of Lisbon.

Like the city, this book contains many different experiences, adventures, anecdotes, offering the reading traveller a variety of perspectives from the points of view of its writers. The stories range from the late nineteenth to the early twenty-first century. Since the strict short story genre as we have come to know it was not the most common form during this period, we have also included a few extracts from travel journals and longer works in this anthology.

We hope the stories and their accompanying photos will whet the reader's appetite and will add to the pleasure of a visit to this beguiling city!

Helen Constantine

Introduction

That we may explore a city through its stories, either in anticipation of travel or as companions along the way, has now become a commonplace. While predictably unreliable tour guides, these stories serve to elicit a sense of place as it was and is. It is atmosphere, that most evanescent of characteristics, which those who venture into a new environment first seek. For in time this aspect of the city may alter or be lost altogether, and we shall be left merely with tales of a vanished and bygone age. Lisbon harbour viewed from the heights of Alfama was blocked by a giant cruise liner when I visited in November 2017. It looks very different in these tales, always more as we would have wished to see it. The more we read of a place we desire to visit, the more the palimpsest of all it once was resurfaces.

These *Lisbon Tales*, presented chronologically, evoke a picture of the city over more than a century. The quality of the writing has been the first criterion in their selection. Some authors are internationally known, others little known in or outside Portugal. Every author offers a snapshot taken from a different angle of a vibrant and historic, cosmopolitan and cultured, alternately bustling and tranquil city. There is much that remains consistent across time—not least in regular glimpses of the coursing River Tagus and the rattling trams—but each writer offers his or her original impressions of this capital.

The short story is not a particularly indigenous literary form in either Portugal or its former colonies, so the present anthology includes a chapter taken from a novella and closes with blogs taken from a live website (subsequently published in book form). There is a chapter from a highly personal Portuguese journey; an excerpted memoir; a philosophical discourse; and something that is at least in part a political tract. Most contributions have not previously been translated and it is somehow fitting that the two unedited exceptions are either by or about Pessoa. The first of these is, predictably, from among the 25,574 writings found in the famous leather trunk after his death, almost entirely unpublished in his lifetime. The second, 'Companions', by Brazilian author and translator Mauro Pinheiro, is a homage to Pessoa, in that he inhabits Pessoa's world as if it were his own.

What caught me unawares when I began researching this anthology was the sheer number of authors who suffered persecution, including exile, under Prime Minister António de Oliveira Salazar's forty-eight-year-long dictatorship. At least one writer, Joaquim Soeiro Pereira Gomes, harnesses writing as an additional medium of protest. His dark tale of living in perilous clandestinity as a Communist Party organizer, gives the gripping account of a man being hunted down, worthy of John Buchan.

I have tried to include the views of the writers who encounter Lisbon, like every tourist, as an incomer. Sometimes it can be hard to tell. Pinheiro does not describe what it feels like to arrive in Lisbon from Rio in the 1980s, but takes a creative leap back eighty years into the city as Pessoa knew it. Magically, his tale reads as if composed contemporaneously. While Pessoa remained almost unpublished and unknown in his lifetime, there is now a vast Pessoa cult and industry. Flocks of tourists follow his steps in the shadow of the castle walls or along the River Tagus, afterward to wend their way to A Brasileira or the Café Martinho da Arcada, where Pessoa consumed life-shortening quantities of alcohol and caffeine.

Orlanda Amarilis was a the third-generation author in her family, born on the Cape Verdean isle of Sta. Catarina, moving to Lisbon only in 1952, aged forty-eight. Amarilis' tale is steeped in her sense of being a perpetual outsider during the period of Cape Verde's long subjection as a Portuguese colony; the colonial residue persisted as an existential condition beyond liberation in the 1970s. Political activity took her across the world, well beyond the cultural elite into which she was born, as she became an international campaigner for peace and human rights. Given the dearth of African publishing houses, her collections of short stories (of which *Cais do Sodré Té Salamansa* is the first) necessarily first appeared in Lisbon following the victory of the Carnation Revolution in 1974. Today Cais do Sodré remains a mainline station with many branches, yet the atmosphere of the eponymous tale is that of stasis, waiting, perplexity as to which is the real destination. The discomfort of the two Cape Verdean immigrants from social extremes who find themselves on the same train, therefore custom-bound to enter into conversation, is a consequence of yet further discrimination. Amarilis very much adopted the short story form as her own, and all three of her ground-breaking collections reprise the theme of the multiple relegations of those marginalized by nationality, gender, and idiom.

The youngest contributor here publishes under the name of Kalaf Angelo. He arrived in Lisbon from Bengoala in 1995, aged 17. Like Amarilis, he came for personal reasons. If Amarilis' writing reveals a diasporic writer, Angelo's blogs—or *crónicas*—display a global one. They are a celebration of cultural fusion, both literary and musical, bringing across the rhythms, sounds, and dances of Africa to interact, integrate, and celebrate with those from earlier centuries, only some of which are European in origin. In contrast, the sounds of *morna* laments from Cape Verde have more in common with Portugal's most famous national *fados*, supposedly of Maghrebi origin.

Kalaf Angelo's vivid renditions of street life indicate something of what has made Lisbon an international go-to city for the young. Over the past twenty years it has become cheaper than Berlin or Prague, and it is far easier to find housing and work-spaces than in London or Paris. Youth is fluid in its capacity to culture-shift and succumb to the charms of Lisbon's old town on its seven hills, each with a distinct identity and panorama, churches and markets, independent shops and galleries, its wide choice of local restaurants and bars. Fresh communities alternate with old-established ones along its steep cobbled streets as newer arrivals take over the tall narrow houses or small factories and warehouses long abandoned by former occupants.

At the opposite end of the historical reach of this selection is Eça de Queiroz, writing at the close of the nineteenth century. Yet he too opposed the formalism of his time with a pioneering realism that has been compared with Proust, Dickens, even Tolstoy (with humour). *Alvez & Co.*, from which this chapter has been taken, is a satirical novella exploring the interplay between interior and external worlds.

Fernando Pessoa's reputation is as a Modernist rather than a Realist, yet it is a philosophical and poetical quest for what it means to be a human being—who we are and who we might become—that most appears to motivate the writing. (Ironically, for one seeking the identity of Everyman, his name—Pessoa—means 'person'.) The excerpt here which, although incomplete, he described as a *conto* follows de Queiroz chronologically yet belongs to another world, in which space and time inhabit their own inner landscapes. Of all the authors in this anthology, he alone offers no actual description of the city of Lisbon, and his 'tale' is the only one to take place just outside the city. It is characteristically free of description of the external world* for his conversation with the elderly Jesuit could have taken place anywhere.

'A Clerical Afternoon' ('Uma Tarde Clerical') comes from the most recent collection of writings rescued from that large domed trunk crammed with manuscripts. Most are in the form of incomplete notes: this is among most entire and I have retained the punctuation and the ellipses of the unedited original, editing out repetitions and

---

* Even when Pessoa, in the guise of a heteronym (an imaginary character) named Alvaro de Campos, 'remembers' Lisbon, he does so with a list of names rather than detailed descriptions. As here, in this fragment of a poem

> *The awakening of Lisbon, later than in other cities*
> *The awakening of Rua do Ouro*
> *The awakening of Rossio Square, at the doors of its cafés*
> *Awakening.....*
> *And in the midst of it all the train station, which never rests*
> *Like a heart that must beat through waking and sleeping hours alike.*

indecipherable phrases. It offers an insight into some of the philosophical preoccupations of Pessoa's time and into his own thinking, including an unusually accurate description of Judaic teaching on the afterlife and his own 'un-conversion' from atheism. It closes with a metaphor that is ostensibly about trams. It would seem that, even in this most abstract (and, in some passages, abstruse) tale, Pessoa cannot escape Lisbon in one of its most typical aspects, one mentioned by so many authors here.

A near half-century of Portuguese fascism, between 1932 and 1974, had an immense impact on those who spoke out. The degree of repression was such that no citizen was left unaffected, for they were forbidden to gather in groups, nor speak—or use a camera– freely in public. José Rodrigues Miguéis came into conflict with the New State, which censored his writing and adversely affected his employment as a lecturer, and he emigrated to New York in 1935. He rarely returned to Portugal and became a US citizen in 1942. With this in mind, it is hard not to read 'The Accident' as a tale that goes beyond a poor worker and an obscurely rich landowner, to focus on the newly built house, as if a parable of the New State, debasing and devouring the lives of those who cannot eat if they do not work to serve it.

Others unwilling—or unable—to go into exile suffered in numerous ways. Soeiro Pereira Gomes' Lisbon alternates between its cobbled streets and alleys and increasingly desperate lodgings, in which the main character seeks to conceal himself and his suitcase of political pamphlets. It is the most overtly party-political of all the tales, given the proximity of this character to Pereira Gomes, himself a member of Portugal's Communist Party's Central Committee. The sensations of never resting or feeling safe, always pursued and on the run, have the stamp of veracity as does the physical suffering of the narrator. Like him, Pereira Gomes was a heavy smoker, and died of lung cancer for which he dared not seek medical attention. Hospital admission would automatically have meant an end to his clandestinity, and perhaps a death sentence still worse than that of his lung disease. Even after his death, his work continued to be published only by the Portuguese Communist Party Press.

Mário Dionísio, born only seven years after Soeiro Gomes (1916), was unable to access a university position, for 'political reasons'. For him the Carnation Revolution of 1974 proved life-transforming, and he lived to see copious academic and literary success. The enigmatic tale 'The Whistler' reads a little differently when one considers that whistling the wrong tune—(if partisan, then literally as well as metaphorically)—was once immediate grounds for repression or reprisal. Until, of course, others around took it up and made it their own.

Mário de Carvalho, like Pereira Gomes, was a clandestine militant in the anti-fascist section of the Portuguese

Communist Party. In 1971, at the age of 27, he was arrested, tortured by the secret police, and imprisoned for fourteen months. Upon release he fled Portugal (overland and on foot), seeking asylum in Sweden. Within months the Carnation Revolution erupted and he returned home to resume political activity, principally in working with trade unions including the Portuguese Writers' Association. In the late 1980s, he lectured at the Escolas Superiores of theatre and cinema and of social communication, and in drama and theatre at Lisbon University. Ostensibly 'Collectors' has little connection with the above, yet it reprises the theme of what happens in the 'new'—post-colonial and post-fascist—world, where bearings are lost and new ones prove elusive. In a continually shifting fantasy world of disappearing islands and erupting land masses, what use is a map? Or, more specifically, how could, would, or should we seek to redraw the world according to our own image and desire?

Both Hélia Correia and Agustina Bessa-Luís operate and manipulate fantasy worlds of mythic dimensions. Their generation was again affected by the Salazar dictatorship, for Correia's father was arrested by the secret police for anti-fascist activity, and she was raised in her mother's hometown of Mafra. Following a first degree in Romance Philology at Lisbon University, she taught in high school, and started publishing poetry and reviews in literary supplements. It was further studies in classical theatre that most marked her literary style thereafter, along with aspects of the Gothic (she cites the influence of Emily Brontë) and of magical realism. 'Metro Zoo' can be read as having elements of all three in the proximity of humans and animals blurring the characteristics of both; the unearthly sense of miasma in the pervasive odours of the zoo; and the increasingly erratic, even anachronistic, actions of the main protagonists. The use of 'pet' names for Sandra; of the term 'handler'—as for an animal—for her pimp; and the textual ambiguities of red paint and a slit throat or of 'entering the lion's den' render her tale sinister beyond what might otherwise have been an everyday story of a poor prostitute living in a malodorous district of the old city.

Like Correia—and like the eponymous fiancé of her tale—Bessa-Luís was an outsider in Lisbon. Similarly to 'Metro Zoo', 'The Fiancé' vividly depicts a city stricken with poverty. It is characteristic of a capital that, before the 1970s, seems hardly to have left the nineteenth century behind, and that is here endowed with a character of its own. A sentence such as 'The town was silent and lifeless... the buildings, with their projecting balconies, resembled old stage sets' echoes Bessa-Luís' close connection to the theatre, for which she wrote, together with the cinema. Her screenplays draw on her own novels, of which she wrote more than forty: *A Sibila* (The Sybil, 1954) references woman's oracular role as seer, and marks a watershed in women's (and feminist) writing, while others focus on the inner lives of women and their proximity to mysticism and the sublime. 'The Fiancé' is more unusual in its focus on the (male) fiancé, and his doomed obsession with attempting to find the morally correct path, even if it must only end in personal tragedy. The mythic dimension derives from her deployment of eternally resonant themes, around making the correct—if tragically irreversible—choices.

Bessa-Luís was born in 1922; Teolinda Gersão almost a generation later, in Coimbra, 1940. Both are renowned feminist authors, and in 'Still Life with Head of Bream' Gersão, like Bessa-Luís, tells her tale from a male viewpoint, even giving the divorced father the narrative voice. Again, Gersão focuses on a contemporary social issue but deploys symbolism alongside realism in addressing the tribulations and insecurities of child-raising shared between a separated couple. Her own life experiences, studying and teaching at universities in Germany and Portugal, living in Brazil and Mozambique, provide ample material for her novels, which she now writes full-time. Four have been adapted for the stage and two short stories as films. Here the visual element is again paramount: the titular painting of a 'still life' of a once-living creature has immediate resonances with a moribund marriage. Gersão takes the association further, portraying a family relationship set in the interstices of a city where a child may be entertained. It is the only tale that is child-centred, like the environments depicted. The banality of visits to park playgrounds and cafés contrasts with the desperate intensity of father–son outings in a city within which a family finds it so hard to coexist.

José Saramago is the author of greatest longevity in the anthology. Born in rural Ribatejo in 1922, his parents left a life of extreme poverty as landless peasants to bring their two sons to the capital in 1924. Although Saramago spent every childhood holiday in Azinhaga with his grandparents so he never felt he lost his rural roots, Lisbon became his home base where he worked as a writer and journalist, latterly as newspaper editor, always in open opposition to the Salazar dictatorship.

Saramago joined the Communist Party in 1969, and remained a member until his death in 2010. He only felt able to dedicate himself to writing fiction full-time in his sixties, when he moved to the Canary Isles with his second wife, the Spanish journalist Pilar del Río. The move was a mark of Saramago's disgust (and disappointment in the democratic regime) on the orders of then Prime Minister Aníbal Cavaco Silva to remove *The Gospel According to Jesus Christ* from the Aristeion Prize shortlist, for causing religious offence. The chapter here taken from his *Journey to Portugal* is not a tale as such. Rather it is a series of tales steeped in the history of Lisbon's cultural landmarks, as well as some of its more personally chosen and recondite byways. Essentially a protracted walking tour, it provides ample material for multiple journeys of exploration. It describes Saramago's 'discovery' or 'recovery', once democratic government prevailed in the 1970s, of his home country, region by region. The style resembles neither his fiction nor his earlier journalism. What results is more like a conversation—or an interaction—between author and his adoptive home city.

Saramago's concluding paragraph to his introduction states that 'a mere tourist guide was what I least wanted *Journey to Portugal* to become'. No more is *Lisbon Tales* intended as one. Rather it is intended as an invitation to readers who may not know Lisbon to become visitors, and a companion to those who would like to revisit either in person or on the page. Also to those who may not be travellers at all, to simply enjoy a voyage of literary discovery.

Amanda Hopkinson

Alves & Co

Eça de Queiroz

Fortunately for Godofredo, in a doorway of the grocer's store across the road stood the elderly Galician who ran errands for him from time to time, often to his father-in-law's house. Godofredo handed him the letter, instructing him to deliver it in person, and not to await a reply. Since he trusted the honesty of the Galician, grown old in the service of the neighbourhood, he added:

'Be sure to place it into his own hand, there's money—a bank note—inside the envelope.'

The old man stuffed the letter deep inside his shirt front, close to his heart.

Then Godofredo positioned himself so as to monitor the letter's progress at a distance.

He watched the old man enter the courtyard of the shabby, four-storey tenement with a second-hand shop on the ground floor. Neto, his father-in-law, had an apartment on the top floor, with a window-box on the balcony. Godofredo maintained his vigil over the door for what seemed like an eternity, but the Galician failed to reappear. He realized he was seized by the fear that Neto might not be at home. What if he only returned after dark, what if he were dining out, or had no intention of coming home before night fell? What was he supposed to do? Wander the streets in the hope his wife might leave their house? The thought left him with a miserable sense of desolation and disorder, as though the natural scheme of things had been ended forever. Suddenly, he spotted the Galician. He must have given the letter to Senhor Neto and come straight downstairs, without awaiting a reply. Greatly relieved, Godofredo began walking aimlessly until, little by little his steps instinctively resumed his daily morning route all the way to his office. He descended the Chiado hillside, pausing for a moment on the Rua do Ouro to study a pistol in Lebreton's shop window. The thought of death crossed his mind, but he had no desire to consider such things at the moment, still less the duel. Later, around seven in the evening, when he was back at his empty house, he would be bound to think about it, about settling accounts with the other man. He continued roaming aimlessly. For a moment he considered going to the Passeio Público, but he feared he might encounter Machado there. He crossed the Terreiro do Paço, along the Aterro, and almost as far as the Rua da Alcântara. He veered to and fro like a sleepwalker, as heedless of the jostling pedestrians as of the loveliness of a summer's eve going down in a blaze of golden splendour. There wasn't a thought in his head: just a tide of ideas, flowing with all kinds of things, memories of his courtship of Ludovina, the day trips they had taken together, and then the manner in which she had reclined against that man's shoulder, the carafe of port placed on the table in front of them. Fragments from her letter persisted in returning to his mind: 'My angel, why ever should I not bear your child?' It was the identical phrase she had used with him, that night when they lay in the warmth of their shared bed, her lips pressed to his... Only now he was glad never to have had a child with such a shameless creature!

It was growing darker, and he thought of going home: he was overcome by a profound exhaustion, the result of so many turbulent emotions, combined with the long walk and the sultry air of that July day. He paused at a café for a moment, and drank a large glass of water: then sat down, leaning his head against a wall, surrendering himself to the enjoyment of this brief respite.

The café was bathed in semi-darkness. A warm evening twilight engulfed the city: each open window was breathing deeply after the heavy heat of the day; one by one the lights came on; and it was possible to watch people pass by, hats in hand already starting to look calmer. He experienced a feeling of pleasure in that twilight, that instant of repose: it seemed to him that his pain was dissipating, dissolving into his bodily inertia, into the shadows of evening. He was overwhelmed with a desire to remain there for good, without the lights ever coming on, without ever having to make another move in his entire life. He was overwhelmed with the thought of death, serene and insinuating, like the caress of a sigh. He truly longed to die. His body had so utterly collapsed under the bitter disappointment he had been forced to confront and all the cruelties yet to come: the return to his lonely home, the meeting with Machado, the rest of the steps to be taken in recruiting seconds—all of it demanded so much effort, appearing as intolerable as giant boulders that his feeble hands would never be able to lift. It would have been delicious simply to stay there, his head resting against the wall. To stay put upon his bench, dead, freed beyond all pain, having departed this life with the silent tranquillity of a light extinguished. For an instant he contemplated suicide. He didn't feel afraid, nor did the notion of actually killing himself scare him. However, the business of having to obtain a weapon, even to take one more step in order to throw himself into the river, were efforts repugnant to him, as demonstrating the complete failure of his will. He wanted to die there, without being obliged to move. Were there just one word, a command whispered low to his heart, ordering him to stop and cool down, he would calmly utter it... And perhaps she would weep and feel his loss... But what of the other man?

At the thought of the other, his resolve returned with a vague flicker of energy, just enough for him to rise to his feet and continue on his way... Yes, that other man would be well-pleased if he were to die tonight. It would come as a perfect relief. For a day or two he would go through the motions of grieving, perhaps he might even feel genuinely upset. And then life would go on: the company would change its name to Machado & Co; the other man would continue going out to the theatre, waxing his moustache, accompanied by his latest mistress. It was so unfair. That other man had ruined their beautiful happiness, he was the one who deserved to die. Machado just ought to disappear; he was the one who deserved to be done away with. That would be more like justice. That was the right way around; the firm would continue to be Alves & Co., and later on he could eventually become reconciled to his wife and life would go on, calm and placid. That was the way it should be. God, in studying the life of first one and then the other man, weighing the vices and virtues of each, should make Machado vanish by planting in his mind the idea of committing suicide.

So, from somewhere between two such crazed fantasies balanced in his tormented soul—between his suicide and that of the other—a new idea surfaced, like a livid flash of lightning between two dark clouds, an idea defined in every detail, seeming to him at once fair and feasible, the most convenient and the only one...

But at that instant, something familiar about the houses he was passing caused him to realise that he was approaching his own front door. He stopped, utterly absorbed by the thought of Ludovina, and stared at his house. A gas lantern was suspended outside that small building between two much taller ones, a model of respectability with its neat, clean frontage, its blue front door and green Venetian blinds. The blinds were down in his own apartment and it was in darkness. Might she still be inside? Had her father come to collect her? A terrible anguish made his heart beat faster. For an instant he longed for her to be there, even contemplated pardoning her, that vacant house so petrified him. But then he felt that, should he have to confront her, he would be cold and constrained; better by far that they should never meet again. Curiosity gradually drew him on to his father-in-law's house at the end of the street. There the tall old building stood, dirty and in need of repair. On the third floor, where his father-in-law ought now to be, open windows breathed in the freshness of evening, and likewise remained in darkness. Neither silent façade offered any kind of response to him, nor anything that might alleviate his disquiet.

He returned home and pushed the front door open. The carpeted staircase slumbered beneath the warm glow of the gas lamp, and the muffled sound of his steps seemed to echo inside an empty cave. From up on the second floor came the sound of a piano, something distant and religious, a piece from *Faust*. The upstairs neighbours were happy, and playing the piano.

The cook came downstairs to open the door, and something about her at once revealed to Godofredo that Ludovina had departed.

In the dining room, a candle was burning on the oil-cloth. He picked it up and entered the bedroom, where he found two suitcases and a trunk, all of them locked.

Yet the room was still strewn with her possessions: beside the bed were her slippers and on the chaise-longue lay the white negligée she had been wearing only that morning. Other objects were still in place—the glass bottles on the dressing table that were so typically hers, and the wooden statue of the Virgin Mary to which she was deeply devoted. He set the candlestick down on the dressing-table, and his pale and aged face stared back at him with an expression of devastation and ruin.

He picked up the candle again, and went into the drawing room. There he encountered the scene of catastrophe.

The fox fur had slipped onto the occasional table beside the sofa where the decanter of port still stood, the stub of the other man's cheroot still beside it. Confronted by that cheroot a dull fury invaded his body. He felt as if he were being buffeted by an iron fist and feared an even greater insult, and swore to become harder, as hard as bronze, never to forgive. He was ready to send on the luggage himself, to see the other man lying dead at his feet, or die in the confrontation.

Nonetheless, he immediately determined to banish all feelings of anxiety and uncertainty. He desired only for his spirits to be governed by a sense of order; for everything at home to revert to its calm and well-regulated way of being. She had left and her luggage would follow that very night. From now on he would be a widower, but the household routine would continue in a serene and orderly manner.

Then he called Margarida.

'Is nobody going to dine in this house tonight? How come it is already late and the table still not set?'

The woman regarded him with a shocked expression that he might consider dining, or that he had returned home to do so. She was obviously on the point of speaking up when he gave her such a stern look that she left with a sidelong glance—within moments, was bustling about zealously laying the table, as though she were seeking absolution for her implied collusion. Then she set out the entire contents of the basket onto the table: the large meat pie, cold ham, and a fruit tart.

While she was doing this Godofredo retreated to his study. Now the idea that had seized hold of him on his walk, the solution that had seemed the only one possible returned and embedded itself in his mind, becoming the focus of all his musings. It amounted to no more than this: he and the other man would simply draw lots as to which of them had to take their own life!

This did not appear to him as in the least excessive, still less extravagant or tragic; on the contrary, it was the sole rational and dignified course of action and the one possible solution. It further appeared to him that he was reasoning it out with consummate detachment. A sword duel between two merchants, both in their shirt-sleeves, trading awkward and pointless slashes until one ended up with an arm wound, seemed little short of ridiculous to him. No less so the option of an exchange of pistol shots which failed to hit their mark, before each of them, followed by his second, ceremoniously returned to his hired carriage. No. Death was the only recourse for such an offence: one loaded pistol, drawn by lot, and fired at point-blank range. But that was hardly realistic. Yet where could they expect to find witnesses who would agree—never mind, willingly—to share the responsibility for such a tragedy? He would be bound to explain the offence to them in vain, for infidelity is a serious matter for the husband in a situation which others might consider a mere mishap that did not merit such blood-letting.

That said, were he the one to die, all well and good, that would spell the end of the matter; but if he were to see the other man fall at his feet, what would become of his life thereafter? He would need to flee, abandon his trading company, start over again seeking his fortune in a foreign land. Where would he go? And he was still left with his principal problem: where on earth would he find seconds for such a course of action? And there would still be scandal and gossip until the truth came out.

Whereas, the other way, all would be easy, secret, decent, without inconveniencing anyone. They would draw lots, and the loser would be obliged to kill himself within the year. If it were he, he would not hesitate for an instant, and would kill himself on the spot. And he had no doubt that Machado would likewise accept!... How could he possibly refuse? He had brought dishonour upon him, Godofredo, and must pay in blood. Just then, he also had an inkling that *he* was going to be the loser... 'If *he* were to die, so much the better,' he thought.

What more of life's pleasures were left to him, alone in that house, always alone, without even the pleasure he had taken in his work, since he no longer wished to spend the money it brought in? Without wasting another second, he must write a curt note to Machado requesting him to come to the office tomorrow, Sunday, at eleven o'clock in the morning... He was just sealing the envelope when Margarida came to let him know that dinner was on the table. He rapidly put his hat on his head, went down the street, and left the envelope at the post box outside the local grocer's, before returning home to reach the dining room where the soup tureen was getting cold—and where Margarida and the cook were plainly astonished at their master's behaviour.

Margarida's presence made him uncomfortable: it seemed to him she could have been an accomplice, or a *confidante*, in the scandal. For a split second, he considered dismissing her. But that would only free up her loose tongue still further, to relay tales of his ruin—adding her own commentaries—in other people's houses. He preferred to retain her, suffer her presence in his home, in order to buy her silence through her fear of dismissal if she did not maintain it...

He had unfolded his napkin and was picking up the soup tureen when there was a forceful ring on the doorbell.

Margarida went down to answer, while he waited with his heart in his mouth. The girl came racing back upstairs and announced, in tones worthy of the annunciation of the arrival of a punitive and vengeful Providence:

'It is Senhor Neto, Sir.'

A Clerical Afternoon

Fernando Pessoa

When the Provisional Government of the Republic dissolved all religious orders, my over-riding priority at the time was to try and discover where my old friend, Father Eusébio and member of the Society of Jesus, might be. I learnt that he had taken refuge in the house of a mutual friend, Vasco Salles. When I could find a suitable day— one fine winter's morning on the first of January on the Republican calendar—I visited my esteemed Jesuit on Vasco Salles' country estate. I found him in indifferent health. And I observed a pronounced apathy in this old member of the Order,* all the more so due to his advanced

* This references other unedited, mainly unpublished, essays or stories: *Leis da Vida; Argumento com o Jesuita; Argumentos contra o Determinismo,* etc. All provide evidence of Pessoa's reading of Sir Thomas Browne's *Religio Medici* (The

years. We spent the day on the estate, returning home only in time for dinner which we took alone, since the owner and his wife had absented themselves to spend a week in the north of the country. Once our early dinner was done, we went to watch the sun set from one of the verandas. The air was fresh, and we both wore our overcoats, with Father Eusébio muffled in his *cachenez*, and we decided to see out the end of day with a philosophical discussion. We had never before had such a protracted conversation; perhaps an obscure intimation that it was to be my last with the elderly Jesuit impelled me to extend our apologetics. For it would not be true to say that ours was a formal discourse. I would merely telegraphically put forward objections to which Father Eusébio responded with brief treatises. My partner's dialectical Catholicism was more than a little interesting.

Between ourselves, a degree of sensitivity indicated the total divergence in our ways of seeing things. I was a free-thinking atheist, a member of the Civil Register;* an apologist for the expulsion of religious Orders and of state intervention in the life of the Church, genuinely desirous that a firm hand be taken to the progressive eradication of what I then considered a way of life compounded of lies,

Religion of a Doctor), his essay on the science of religion, also his spiritual testament and a psychological self-portrait.

* Founded on 5 August 1895, heavily influenced by Freemasonry, its objectives were to combat clericalism and religious fanaticism and to defend secular government.

hypocrisy, greed, corruption, and cruelty. He was, it goes without saying, the Jesuit Father Eusébio Quelhas. My principal aversion to the Church was as a result of its doctrines. Cruelties, hypocrisies, corruptions—the effect of all this being the fundamental rubric of a *lie*, with *false* theories and doctrines. Modern science—I then believed— had destroyed all that the Church had once maintained— from the immortality of the soul to free will; from the existence of hell to the possibility of miracles. Beliefs that seemed to me so entirely absurd there was no conceivable defence for them. I held it as indisputably clear and evident, beyond all dispute in the realms of reason or logic, that such Catholic theories were completely impossible to substantiate...

All hypocritical moralizing was derived from this. The hypocrisy—to spell it out—was derived from a false corruption of the truth. No doubt this was unconscious, truth was killed by an evidently vast moral corruption, accommodated by a knowingly scandalous desire for temporal and earthly dominion. All this is evil, I thought, false, erroneous, and infamous; and in being false, erroneous, and infamous, it is plain in the eyes of wisdom and knowledge. Considering that afterwards I completely changed my mind and so scandalized many in the Association for the Civil Register, that I set aside my loathing of religion and the Church, without so much as granting my former colleagues the satisfaction of adopting the faith, or of defending, judging, or owing them an account of how I turned from being an atheist to becoming an indifferent, anticlerical defender of tolerance, certain in my knowledge...rooted in science, uncertain as to the degree of falsehood of something, dubious as to the strength of truth that science contains, somewhat sadly I surrendered my will to see others left to persist in their own beliefs, and to enjoy their freedom. I left behind me all those false certainties, and in abandoning them I lost all grounds for loving or loathing things, this and that, in order to ascertain what was true and what false. Today I know that the human spirit is more fantastical than I had assumed, and that the truth is more obscure than I had thought, and examining and advancing is all, for it is as easy and as sure to defend one thing as another in this world because, as I obtained the proof on the clerical afternoon of which I shall tell you, either there is something real in our world, along with, not truths but the defence of truths; not certainties but arguments that, faith in God weighs the same as a lack of faith in God and, being so, it is as logical to say that hell is a matter of fact as to see it as absurd. I used to believe that one should believe in whatever one wanted to. I don't hate one priest nowadays, any more than I feel sympathy for another; these days I tend more towards tolerating the priest, all the more so for having been so unfair on him for so long, so much more than the atheist for, without justification, I was for so long and helped others to become.

Without having been converted by his arguments, but having become unconverted by my own, I was taught all this and more one late-January afternoon by the Jesuit Father Eusébio Quelhas.

II

'No, my son,' said Father Eusébio, 'I won't now get to write that book of mine...I am old and, more than old, in poor health. I won't last long. The things of this world no longer attract me with the power they once had. Others will write them, others will write them. There are plenty of others to defend the faith.'

'Could you give me some idea of your book?'

'I shall start by demonstrating,' said Father Eusébio, 'that knowledge of all scientific or scientifically philosophical methods cannot bring us to this or that concept or conclusion regarding the truth.

'It is difficult, so difficult, my dear young friend, to mount an argument...Between the soul of the unbeliever and the believer alike there is a qualitative difference, impossible to bridge even in the imagination. The whole way of facing the world and everything in it is utterly different from within the soul of a believer, so to speak, than from that of a non-believer, in its most elementary and fundamental spiritual composition. And believe it my good friend, however well you understand me, even so you cannot comprehend entirely what is going on. No, no, no; I am not saying this to be unpleasant to you—as you know, I am incapable of contemplating behaving in such a manner. It is because it is the truth, the truth.

'It is just as difficult to integrate our spirit with the ambience of the past. Could I affirm, with the conviction of telling the truth, that there is no anonymous faculty possessed of miraculous effect? Could I guarantee such a thing? No I could not, I could not.

'Science has good legs, but faith, my friend, has wings. However fast science may run, faith will always catch up, assisted by the wings in our heels. And when it can run no further, when feet bleed and legs buckle... with exhaustion, faith beats its wings and takes flight.'

'Flying also exhausts you.'

'Then it is time to return to earth and resume running.'

*   *   *

'Yes indeed,' said the Jesuit. 'But the fact of the matter is this. If we deny Nature or whatever it is that generates us, places us here through the mediation of natural laws, intelligence and reason, it implicitly causes us to affirm our absolute superiority over nature herself (as we like to call it). Being more aware than any other animal—so far as we know—deliberately denying nature, we believe ourselves superior to Nature itself—there can be no more ridiculous and presumptuous anthropomorphism than this, my dear friend. Follow the logic of my argument. Seeing as we are essentially aware beings, the more so when we reason and occupy ourselves with science, implies one of two things: we possess awareness either through inferiority or superiority. It is through our own sense of superiority that we fall into the error of attributing to ourselves a superiority over Nature; we concede to her no degree of consciousness, for by doing so we would thereby grant her an infinite status, so to say (because *status* and *infinity* are incompatible terms). And if Nature were superiority and so infinitely aware—then, my dear friend, we encounter God.'

'And the alternative hypothesis?'

'Ah, are we now saying that awareness is inferiority? Yes, yes. In which case, leave aside intelligence—an essential part of awareness—as the criterion for truth. Once the supremacy of reason is removed, then every argument for the entire rationalist cause is downed. Because, at the very least, once faith is surrendered to the arbitrariness of each one of us without any possible refutation or logical defence; then I am free to believe in God as I like, without the need for intervening arguments.'

'Then yes, then yes, but it's not about so much for the sea, so much for the land... Nor does it amount to 8 or 80. One has no need to apologize for acknowledging neither supremacy nor the invalidity of awareness.'

'So what other hypothesis…?'

'Any hypothesis which is part-way between the two…
there must be a mid-point between what you…present
me with, Padre.'

'Now let's see. Midway?…

'Memory permits psychic activity to persist. From
which we can *retain* the *abstract* with the *concrete, strange
as they both are.* They scarcely exist in order to maintain
the unity of the spirit.*

'"Unconscious thought" is like a pebble once it has
been thrown up into the air; its height depends on the initial abstraction.†

'Intuition or inspiration constitutes an instinctive
approach, independent of the thought processes in our
brain cells, primarily forged by consciousness.…

'The soul is real and absolute, rooted *sub specie eter-
nitatis*…'

'Does an individual in a state of automatism therefore
remain incapable of abstraction? Of *original* abstraction.
Yes. He does not lose the abstract ideas that run through
his memory. But he loses the *will*—isn't it curious that an
epi-phenomenon should count for so much?

---

* This sentence is unclear in the original [note from Ana Maria Freitas, editor
of the Portuguese edition].

† Another original marginal note: ('*And the poems of lunatics?*) [There is also
an expression *doidos de pedras*—mad as stones—roughly equivalent to 'stir
crazy' or 'mad as a hatter', 'a wet cat', or 'a box of frogs'.]

'If one assumes that man should essentially be defined by consciousness, and consciousness is essentially abstract, everything gains a new aspect. And the question of free will, when seen in a new light, becomes clearly defensible and comprehensible....

'We are capable of abstraction, able to confront facts and motives objectively considered. This is a human characteristic.

'This is why the Church recognizes man as a rational animal. (And it is why man has the faculty of language.)

'This is also why we say that God gave free will to man.'

The abstract cannot be thought by the material-in-itself (the brain). Only the brain—a material thing—can have concrete ideas.*

Every being has the capacity for thought, and is conscious according to its nature; such a limited entity cannot conceive of the limitless. (The human soul, however, thinks to a limitless degree....)

Being possessed of free will, there is also responsibility, blame and sin, from which punishment can derive. All these ideas are linked so closely that sin could in part be diminished by the momentary influence of passions that differ in intensity for each individual. There are two levels of punishment: purgatory and hell, the former for the somewhat guilty and the latter for those irredeemably so.

---

* This remains an uncorrected contradiction. Punctuation, Latin spellings, ellipses are retained as in the original notes.

'Kindly permit me to tell you that current thinking on the subject of hell is somewhat erroneous. In general, even religious ministers fail to explain the concept very clearly; they return to exaggerated and pagan representations which provoke hilarity among unbelievers and enemies of the Church and which, it is a pity to have to say, does not instil the terror it ought in believers. Obviously, for rudimentary believers, any proper explanation would need to be more simply expressed in order for them to understand.

The concept of hell is always expressed by fire. This notion of fire is Judaic, and we have to interpret it as Jews would, before we can appreciate how Christianity and the Church have subsequently interpreted it and, in reality, even without providing an adequate explanation, they now understand it. It is commonplace to consider that in Judaism, as in our own sainted religion, fire signifies *torture*, by which "eternal agony" we understand to burn in eternal suffering, in the eternal fire... This is an error. Fire is *not what* tortures by burning, but rather consumes and destroys, reducing all to nothing. Hence the Judaic saying that God takes pleasure in good, while evil *dies utterly and forever.**

*   *   *

* In the left margin of the original mss., alongside this paragraph, is written: *How to prove this—(Like Drummond?) Surely not.* Henry Drummond (1851–97) was a Scottish writer who analysed the links between science and religion in his *Natural Law in the Spiritual World*, where he defended the scientific principle of continuity across the natural and spiritual world.

Man is egotistical by nature, capable only of desiring the good of others for his own good…

Without sanction from above, why should man behave altruistically, or why should anything matter more to him than his pleasure or passions?

Man has his duties to society, for without society, what would he be? What evil would result from avoiding these obligations? Assuming the hypothesis that life ends in death without reward for good actions or sanction for evil ones, why should a man desist from his bad acts in order to practise* good ones, since by undertaking a good action he risks no harm to himself, and in not doing so he risks no punishment?

I am not saying that a real criminal finds his chosen career arduous. Rather, I am referring to a total egotist who is not a criminal as such. Who just goes through life without the least concern for others and without engaging in theft or murder.

Hedonism is the only philosophy for one who has no religion.

And what of conscience? An awareness of conscience is the final product of centuries of moralizing. And how did this moralizing come about? How else than by the infiltration of religious ideas, gradual because egotism is possessed of

* More usually expressed as *homo homini lupus* (a man is a wolf to another man).

immense force, uncertain because instincts are so dominant. This is virtue, the moral material that stands against "original sin". Man as man is essentially a sinner, *homine lupus.'*

*   *   *

Even sociology cannot escape the evidence of the hand of providence. For it depends on whether one sees in social evolution the operation of a rigid law and its order or not, and either way it means we admit the possibility of such a thing, or something similar to it, in human life. Therefore we need to see a distinction between forms of human social life, and human social life in and of itself. Once this is acknowledged, one is obliged to admit ipso facto, free will, since we are clearly assuming a particularly distinctive feature of mankind in comparison with other biological entities. Since this distinction is acknowledged as a consequence of chance, then with it, so is free will.

Yet I still apologize in admitting all this. In general we assume that social life is governed by laws, just like any other form of life, but hardly more complex, the more hidden the direct lines or directions of these fundamental laws may be. Even so one has to admit that the hand of providence, the *external* cause, provides direction and orientation for social life from outside society, for example through nature in general and forces beyond nature. For the problem may be posed in two possible ways. The case is *how* to achieve [the implementation of] these laws. My dear friend knows full well that there are two opposite principal arguments in respect of social life. One is the theory that what is essential is the individual, the other that what is essential is the social being. In addition there is another theory to reconcile the two. With regard to its achievement we must, according to the theory that all social life is achieved by individuals, [concede] that history is that of great men and the sociology of history is the study of the conditions of their emergence; or else, according to the other theory, the life of societies is essentially something which transcends individuals, great and small, who float more or less visibly on the surface of social currents.

* * *

'Once upon a time, there was a man who was waiting for a tram to arrive.

He was waiting for a tram with a signboard indicating his destination.

He was waiting a long time, as if there were never going to be another tram.

At long last a tram appeared at the end of the street, he saw it was coming toward him, and it was the first. It did not have a signboard indicating its destination on the front, but it was the first to come and he had been waiting so long. It was neither full nor empty; it was travelling neither fast nor slowly; it was simply the first tram ever since he had been waiting for one. He hesitated, but let it go by.

Soon afterwards another tram appeared. It was not the first tram, since the first one had already gone. It was travelling slowly and empty. The man was tempted to board the empty tram that was travelling slowly and would doubtless be so comfortable, particularly since he had been waiting so long for it. The signboard did not show his destination, but it would be heading in the same direction, and travelling in an empty tram is always pleasant. He hesitated, but he let it go by.

Soon afterwards, when he was even more tired, he suddenly saw another tram which reached him where he stood before coming to a halt. It was full, and had been travelling fast. It too did not display a signboard indicating his destination. Whoever boarded it would therefore not be able to go where he wanted to. The man hesitated, before letting it go by. Then he saw another tram coming, but even at a distance the man recognized the guard and the conductor, standing and making small talk together [on the running board of] the first carriage. The tram had no signboard in front, because it was returning to the depot. The man hesitated, because he knew the guard and conductor, and travelling with them would amount to the same thing as travelling with his own destination indicated on the signboard. But, once having hesitated, he did not hesitate, and let that one too go by.

In the end, when the man was tired of being tired, he saw a tram with his destination on its signboard. It was neither full nor empty, travelling neither fast nor slowly, and carrying neither people known nor unknown to him. For him alone it bore the signboard indicating his destination. The man did not hesitate, and boarded the tram. This was how he reached his home, for this was the tram to take him home.

This man is a great lesson. For he knew to wait for the tram that bore a signboard with his destination on it.

But how is this man a great lesson to us all? All of us, when we wait for a tram, do as he does. But how many of us do as he does if we are waiting for life? How many of us possess the strength to wait for the tram that bears precisely…'

It seemed to me, although I may have been mistaken, a mere effect of the light that, in uttering these words, and in raising his hands to the heavens, Father Quelhas swiftly winked an eye at infinity.

Lost Refuge

Soeiro Pereira Gomes

For comrade João,* who inspired this story.

Without putting down the suitcase, he waited for the tram to approach. He felt he was nearing the end of the riskiest phase of the task, fraught with dangers. What a relief it would be when he finally reached home!

He was exhausted, sweaty, and terribly thirsty. Still, he tried to assume an amiable expression, as if announcing to everyone waiting on the platform: 'Lovely morning, isn't it? Don't worry about the suitcase... It's full of clothes and doesn't weigh a thing.' Of course people noticed there was one more competitor for the empty seats on the tram, but otherwise paid no attention to the skinny, poorly dressed

---

* Pseudonym used in clandestinity by comrade Dias Lourenço.

young man, whose eyes glinted nervously beneath the lowered brim of his hat.

When the tram came to a halt, Abel tried to board together with his suitcase, but, on finding himself unable to manage, let it fall onto the platform. Two kindly gentlemen came to his rescue. He tipped his hat in thanks, and then shuddered on noticing their sinister faces, as one urged him:

'Don't worry. You can stow the suitcase over here.'

The voice was mellifluous and deliberate.

'Thank you very much,' said Abel.

He pushed his way through, settling himself on a seat at the front, nearest the exit, struggling to maintain a composed and friendly expression. 'Relax, relax. Don't behave like a scared rabbit. And those men, unfriendly or not, were no doubt harmless. Why be suspicious if they politely and spontaneously lend a helping hand?'

Feeling calmer, he lit a cigarette and, after calculating the distance between himself and the door, ran his eye over the other passengers. 'That girl with the snub nose... she looks like fun...' But the attempt to distract himself from his worries didn't last. The two men were standing at the back and appeared to be watching him. 'Hell!' At that moment he could have sworn that he'd intercepted a secret signal relayed to another passenger. Things were turning ugly.

He considered getting off at the next stop, since it would mean serious trouble if he arrived home with a load of police on his tail. But to alight there, between the cemetery and an uninhabited wasteland....What direction could he take without them noticing such a large suitcase in his hand, one which the two men already knew was heavy? He could drop the suitcase and run...no, never! To flee would be a betrayal—as his friends always told him, you have to keep going until the last throw of the dice. Abandoning the suitcase without putting up the least resistance would be to betray those who'd placed their trust in him: his comrades-in-arms, his Party.

The tram was approaching its terminus...It stopped. Abel didn't rush to get off. He grabbed hold of the suitcase and, walking upright and purposefully, as if it were neither invaluable nor heavy, overtook the two men, who appeared to hesitate over which way to go. A few steps further on he turned aside slightly, as if to tie his shoelace, and saw he was being followed by the passenger on the front seat, the one who'd picked up the signal. Abel quickened his stride, took the first corner then, acting decisively, ducked into a doorway, bounding up the stairs to the first floor. He paused there, panting heavily. Through the transom window, he watched the other man go by with his head held high, as if trying to pick up the scent.

'Are you looking for someone?' asked a woman, pausing as she scrubbed the first floor landing.

'Yes...I mean: is this where Mr. X lives?' (He gave a name at random.)

'No, it's not. I know all the tenants. Now let me see. That one on the right...'

'Thank you very much,' interrupted Abel. 'Good-day.'

He went back down the stairs, checked the nearly deserted street and, after doubling back around the corner, headed for home at a smart pace.

When he reached his room, his refuge, he threw himself down onto the bed with relief and satisfaction. He might yet get away with it this time! Though he'd lost a night's sleep, he didn't feel tired but his feet hurt and were no doubt covered in burst blisters under the socks that, as always, stuck to his skin. Even after three months at that task—going to collect the propaganda material, before distributing it—he still hadn't developed calluses on his feet like his other comrades, who put up with miles of walking. It's true! Three months since he'd plunged into this clandestine lifestyle! Ninety days of struggle, escaping fascist informers, sharing an unfamiliar, yet still welcoming home in the narrow room which comprised his whole world in terms of rest, study, and, intermittently, sleep. He was very fond of that room with its low ceiling and damp-stained walls, with an iron bedstead without a mattress or bedspread on one side, and a rough-hewn table, standing next to the suitcase on the other; as well as a window that overlooked the backs of the buildings, but from where you could just see, in the distance, a small slip of the river.

In the evenings, when the sun mirrored reflections on the dirty broken rear windows and tenants returned home from work, jostling in the city streets, Abel would lean out over the windowsill and allow himself to participate in the alternately happy or sad moods of his neighbours. Men in shirtsleeves occupied themselves in mending old chicken coops, or diligently watered the withered loquat tree that would never bear fruit, while women set their tables on narrow balconies if the weather was good, and nippers hopped around like famished birds.

They liked him, the nippers. From a distance, they showed off their pathetic toys and games, blowing kisses and firing pretend gunshots in his direction; he responded by pulling comical faces that had them choking with laughter. At night, nothing could distress him more than to hear fierce reprimands cut short by the sudden sharp wail of a child. He would lean out of the window and try to guess what was happening beyond the darkness. On one occasion he went as far as to reproach a neighbour who was hitting Luisinha, a blonde girl who reminded him of his youngest sister.

'Why are you beating a little girl like that? Maybe she is in pain and that's why she's moaning? Leave her be.'

His words came out roughly, and the woman replied:

'Who are you to tell me what to do? A right meddler we have here! Mind your own business!'

Who *was* he…? In truth: nobody. His life was no different to that of any proletarian in his country, any of those hungry for bread and justice; it was pretty much like the life of the woman herself, at her wits' end, who knows why. Misery, it was, there for all to see. 'Ah, but one day… one fine morning the sun shall shine brightly… yes, the sun…'

* * *

He awoke, startled by the noise of the bell. 'Two short rings and one long one… Could it really be that?' He went to peer through the peephole, before opening the door.

'Ah, so it's you. You gave me a fright, you know!'

'Have you sorted through the material yet?' asked the other man apprehensively.

'Not yet. I fell asleep as soon as I got in…'

'Then grab the suitcase and clear out of here. This neighbourhood's being watched by the fascist police. Rent a room as far away as possible. Check the small ads in the papers. The comrade in charge wants you to meet him at 4 o'clock, and bring along the suitcase with the material from the provinces. You know the place. Report back tomorrow morning at 8 o'clock. You got all that?'

Abel had sat down on the bed, bewildered. He still hadn't connected the present situation with what happened on the tram. He began raising objections:

'But I've got to wash my feet first... Look at the state of them! Then I need to put together my clothes and the rest of my belongings... It'll take me a little while.'

'Forget about your feet, comrade. The police are just around the corner! And what belongings have you got to put together? Nothing.'

'You're right', murmured Abel, glancing around the room, as if saying farewell, and then at the backs of the buildings where he could hear Luisinha chirping.

His companion rapidly packed some clothes while Abel wrote a warning note for his house mates who were out at work. As they left, the man suddenly remembered:

'We still haven't figured out a route. Where do you plan on going?'

'Best to head for Vale Escuro, the dark valley.'

His friend agreed.

'Good luck. And hang in there!'

Abel grasped the man's hand firmly and headed straight for the road leading to Azinhaga do Vale, casting intermittent glances back over his shoulder.

Vale Escuro was a narrow plain between two steep hillsides. Only the owners of a rundown farm by the side of the road attempted to cultivate its hard grey earth, while the city resisted taking over its slopes. Used as a rubbish dump, the valley was also shared by those booted out by the city-dwellers: pedlars, who disrupted early mornings

with their cries; unlicensed prostitutes and backstreet busk-
ers; rag-and-bone men who competed with the dogs over
rubbish bins; kids too—city orphans, nobody's children—,
living together in shacks made of wood or tin, or under
old bits of canvas strung between a couple of decrepit olive
trees.

This time, Abel paid no attention to the wasteland of
misery at the heart of the city. He wanted to find refuge
and catch some rest, fast. After scanning the ads page in a
newspaper, he finally knocked at a door he'd picked out.

'Have you a room here to let?'

'Please come on in.'

It was a dark and dingy room, with a single shuttered
window overlooking the back yard. Gone was the slip of
river, the comfort of a welcoming home, Luisinha's laughter! But the landlady seemed kind.

'The rent's two-hundred *escudos*', she said.

'That high?'

The woman blamed the 'black market' and a monthly
pension which couldn't feed her for a week. (She was the
widow of a civil servant.) Abel hesitated. But the case
weighed like lead and his feet were killing him...So he
stayed.

Then, lying on the bed, he realized he'd need to buy
another suitcase, or a trunk with locks this time, somewhere he could stash the clandestine newspapers, because

the one he owned hadn't so much as a key. 'But what if, while he was away, the landlady searched the suitcase? Maybe she wouldn't. She didn't look like a busybody. Either way, he mustn't be gone long.'

He went out in search of a suitcase. But when he returned, a short while later, the woman approached him with a troubled expression...

'Excuse me, you still haven't told me what you do or where you're from. Where do you work?'

'I'm a travelling salesman', answered Abel adding, by way of extra information, the name of a region not too far from his own. 'I also do a bit of writing...'

'Is that so?' She paused, before adding: 'I'm sorry, but it's important to know who you're bringing into your home. I've enough problems as it is.'

The young man did his best to allay her suspicions; but he could already sense that an irreparable break had taken place. He went to look at the suitcase, and found it had been tampered with. A curse escaped his lips. And he felt downhearted for the first time that day, overcome by events, and choked back his tears.

A short while later, however, and he was still there, motionless and crestfallen. Spread out in front of him, the newspapers spoke of a people oppressed by fascism and a homeland in danger; they argued that it was necessary to fight and to win. For a moment he could picture the eyes of his comrades, heavy with shadows from late nights at the clandestine press; he watched their feverish hands, running across the reams of paper, typesetting the articles. And he heard—could have sworn that he heard—the whisper of thousands of voices, insistently crying out: 'Forward! Forward!'

Then Abel rose resolutely to his feet. He told the landlady he'd be back in the evening, but had no intention of returning. And again he faced the uncertainty of finding refuge and the dangers of being out on the street. When he arrived at the meeting place there was no sign of his senior comrade. It was too late!

He picked up the latest edition of the paper and once again went up and down staircases, clinging to banisters, dragging the suitcase. Finally, he thought he'd managed to find a safe and welcoming room. Coming from deep inside the house, he could hear a radio playing the melodious chords of a particular song he'd heard before, though he wasn't sure where. It calmed his nerves. But when he went to put away his hat and the suitcase, the landlady told him:

'You'll have to go without the door key for tonight.'

'That doesn't matter.'

'But if you prefer, there's still enough time for me to go collect it from Aljube gaol.'

He looked taken aback and the landlady explained:

'It's just that the guest who was staying here was arrested yesterday, you know, for political reasons.'

Abel was petrified. It took him a couple of moments before he could speak without giving himself away:

'Would it be possible to hold the room till tonight? You see I still have to drop the samples in this suitcase off at the warehouse. I'm a travelling salesman...'

'That's absolutely fine.'

Abel ran down the stairs. 'No way could the place not be under surveillance!' At the same moment a shiver ran through him. On the landing near the entrance, a suspicious figure melted seamlessly into the shadows. He observed it was a short man, his hat pulled down over his eyes, who began to follow him as soon as he stepped outside. Abel quickened his pace, attempting to glide between the pedestrians who were crowding the pavements. It was a time of day when people streaming home from work overflowed onto streets brimming with life. Many were carrying packets or carrier bags in their hands, but no-one had anything like the heavy suitcase Abel was dragging behind him, all the while attempting to pass unnoticed.

The man was still there behind him, clinging to the wall like a lizard. Abel glimpsed him out of the corner of one eye, while affecting to study window displays; at his back he could feel the chill of the man's presence. He turned the first corner and broke into a run. He had to reach another road before the policeman appeared. But when he looked back, it was no longer just the one man but two, maybe more, who seemed to be following him. One of them was short with a hat tugged down over his eyes.

Now the sweat was pouring down his face; his shoes squeezed his feet like pincers; and a sharp stitch had developed under his ribs. But he clenched his teeth and a sense of determination gripped his whole being. 'I shan't let go of this suitcase! I'll deliver the newspapers the comrades entrusted me with!'

He lengthened his stride as far as he could, went down another street, turned one and then another corner. The suspicious faces continued to stare fixedly at him, forever there at a set distance behind him! A young street-seller suddenly yelled out the name of a newspaper right beside him, making Abel jump. Then a woman berated him for barging into her.

'You're drunk!' he heard her say.

But the insult was immediately overcome by the obsession that was tormenting him: 'No, I shan't let go of the suitcase!' He felt an urge to shout defiantly at his enemies, at the entire city. 'I'm not afraid, you scoundrels! I'll take you all on, one at a time!' But he kept moving painfully forwards, the suitcase knocking against his legs and the sweat drenching his underwear.

Further ahead, he was caught in the bright lights of a car. Abel was dazzled. 'Was it the police? Could he be trapped in an ambush?' He still hadn't noticed that night had fallen on the city and that thousands of lights had been switched on. His only concern was to rid himself of the dark moving shadows following him wherever he went; and from the suspicious eyes that looked him up and down, bringing a lump to his throat like a hangman's knot. The long, long city appeared never-ending. And not a single door open to him! Ah, if only he could drag himself to a dark corner where he could hide...

He continued down more streets that were dimly lit and almost deserted. Suddenly he lost his footing and found himself tumbling on the uneven surface. He steadied himself and looked around. The faint light of many streetlamps stretching into the distance allowed him to make out the contours of Vale Escuro, plunged in shadows and silence. He remained like this for a while, listening intently. Gradually, his anguish began to subside. He couldn't even feel his feet. Even worse was the sharp pain stabbing his stomach. How long had had it been since he'd eaten?

He pulled his coat collar tightly around his neck; the suitcase would have to serve as a pillow. 'What did his hunger matter to him now? He would deliver the newspapers as arranged; he would finish the job. And one day... one fine morning the sun shall shine brightly... yes, the sun... Aha...!'

The Accident

José Rodrigues Miguéis

The house is starting to take shape, the blood-red window frames already installed, awaiting just a final lick of paint once the panes of glass are in. It is a spacious home for rich occupants, the type of house commonly referred to as a palace, with numerous floors, a gigantic cellar, a terrace enclosed by a railing, altogether occupying almost an entire block. It could have accommodated ten families. The design is classical and pompous, heavily ostentatious, a kind of over-worked baroque. For over a year mountains of building materials have been accumulating there, and yet no one knows for certain when it may be completed. Such an opulent house appears to have an insatiable appetite for growing.

There is a plot of adjacent land, on which the flower garden is to be laid out, with terraced lawns, palm trees, rose bushes and winding pathways (as intricate as they are pointless), and—in all probability—an artificial lake with a fountain and gold fish, and a surround decorated with shells. For the time being, there is little beyond mud and puddles, with building materials and all sorts of rubbish piled here and there. Three olive trees still resist and remain standing, reminders of an earlier period of orchards and kitchen gardens, singing streams and happy picnics.

On Sundays, families stop by. They are easily impressed, and stand in the muddy road outside and gawp: 'They must be building a masterpiece here!'

Some even politely, cap-in-hand, ask permission to pay a visit. And the men of the family wax lyrical while indicating the ceiling with a cane or an umbrella, assessing the astonishing thickness of the walls:

'They don't have walls like that even up at the Moors' Castle! What we have here should last for centuries. They don't make walls this solid anymore, not like they used to! What a fine construction!'

(The good bourgeois, however ephemeral himself, appreciates those things that will outlast him, that promise to endure forever.)

Overnight the construction site is guarded by a tall skinny man, with something of a furtive look about him.

He whiles away the hours sitting with his back against a wall and his feet at the edge of a campfire, coaxing the latest popular tunes from his harmonica. They are accompanied by an irregular and agonised rhythm, projecting something sinister of his own into the dark night. They say he bears two corpses on his back, belonging to a man and a woman whom one night he surprised in the midst of taking their illicit pleasure. A particular contempt for the night and for death may well be what make him the perfect night watchman. He has a special 'friend', a stout blonde, who is consumed by jealousy. After dinner and seated beside the fence, she rains insults and provocations down on him across the campfire. She wants him to give her a beating, the supreme proof of love. But he continues coaxing restless tunes from his harmonica, his back to the wall and his gaze lost among the stars, offering no response. Human life is fragile.

At the crack of dawn, the building contractor makes a tour of the site, half a cheroot clamped between his teeth, his stubble unshaven, wearing a soft hat crumpled at the back, his trousers rolled up, and in a constant state of agitation. Rain is bucketing down and the house is mired in mud. He carries an open umbrella and the cotton ties securing his underpants are showing. The man never pauses, slipping and slithering as he jumps heavily through the claggy clay of the terrace, tripping over building matter, issuing expletives mixed with saliva, blackened by

chewed cheroot. The house is his nightmare. The workmen are distributed through countless rooms; they include
stonemasons, bricklayers, plasterers, carpenters, painters,
electricians, plumbers...

'These windows don't have latches. The rain has flooded
the whole room! You, watchman, you'll be out on your ear
if you leave my windows open again!'

'But the window panes aren't in yet!'

'Well, so they obviously should be! What's the glazier
up to? Why hasn't he arrived yet?'

Everything seems to be running backwards. Every day
the plans get changed, on the basis of new inspections and
suggestions. His thundering tones reverberate throughout
each room and up through the floors like a tempest. Not
to mention the black spittle from the perpetually unlit
half-cheroot. Men are at work in every corner of the building: kneeling, crouching, upright, standing on step-ladders,
or lost in the roof rafters. They are silent, obstinate, and
resigned as they refine, retouch, and beautify the rich man's
house, some man they know nothing whatever about. Not
once do you hear a voice raised in song.

An old woman comes by daily. She looks quite comical
as she hops over mud and puddles so as not to wet her
shoes. They must already have had all of ten years' wear,
dating back to the days of her late husband. She is the
mother of one of the bricklayers there. She arrives wearing

her black cotton mantilla; a small jacket which in former years had also been black but which is now bronze; her skirt darned and patched, and carrying an umbrella and a hot meal in her basket. It was as if her son were still at school. There's no one else in her life, he is all she has. At first his workmates made fun of the lad, laughing out loud at him. Over time they came to like the old woman, having grown accustomed to her.

She arrives punctually before the whistle sounds for the midday break, sometimes soaked to the bone. She enters by the wrought iron gate in the garden fence (unpainted and still the colour of red lead) and leans against the wall, below the enormous glass canopy over the room where the owners will one day have their meals. She adjusts her mantilla, beneath which a yellowed lock of hair keeps escaping, and waits humbly, huddled against the wall, her basket beside her, arms crossed in front of her, clutching her umbrella. The scaffolding shelters her from the downpour, and the wall screens her from the south-westerly wind. There she waits for the foreman to blow his whistle, and her son to emerge. Sometimes she bends down to pick up a piece of wood or a fistful of pale yellow shavings from the ground: tremulously, without letting anyone notice her, as if they were straws of gold.

The foreman sounds his whistle—always after midday has struck, as if his watch ran more slowly at that hour—and the men file out down the back stairs when the weather is fine, or gather in groups around the rooms, if it rains. The boy leaves the others and goes to sit at the old lady's feet. She spreads a cloth out over a plank or a stone so as to avoid dirtying her skirt, and sits down. She opens her basket and the two of them eat together. Occasionally they might exchange a few words. The boy is not a talker. No one knows what they say to each other, the widowed mother and her bricklayer son.

He is a good, hard-working lad. He doesn't smoke or hang around bars, and the two of them live in a shack at Pote d'Agua, on the minimal wage he scrapes from the stones. She earns a bit from collecting rags to weave into rugs and put towards paying the rent. That's as much as anyone knows about them. Nothing more, for they're poor, the same as all the rest of the poor. When lunch is done, he casts an eye over the newspaper. Then she returns the pot and two plates to the basket, while her son takes a last swig from the bottle. The old woman rearranges her stray lock of hair and her mantilla, then departs. Comical as ever, she hops, over the mud and puddles on her skinny ankles, so as not to wet the shoes dating back to the days of her late husband, dressed all in faded black, her little wicker basket in one hand, and her umbrella clutched to her chest.

That was over a year ago. By now no one even notices her any more. Some workmen bring in their midday meal wrapped in newspaper, or else in a lunch or a toolbox. Others cook for themselves outside on a fire made of wood chips and shavings. The old woman is their only visitor, arriving just before the whistle, and waits leaning against the wall, worn and humble. She is there through almost two winters, while the building work seems to go on forever. So much the better. It provides the workman's livelihood: 'Thanks be to God.' And she waits. It seems almost as good as a job in the Town Hall. Her late husband, he worked in the slaughterhouse for over thirty years.

And she repeats once more, in gratitude: 'Lord our God, save all those who offer work to the poor.'

'Know who snuffed it t'other day?' asks the master carpenter, straining to hang a door on its hinges. 'Here, lend me a hand.'

'No I don't, Sir. Who was it?'

Luis, the house painter lays his brush on the window sill and goes over to give the carpenter a hand.

'Well, it was only the owner of all this.'

'Owner of all what?'

'Owner of this construction job, of all this, man! Now hold it still for a moment, just like that. I mean the big boss who ordered this house to be built. Now the whole lot belongs to his heirs.'

'Oh, those fellows we've seen come round here in the car every morning, sticking their noses in? A bad lot, you can tell. They did all right out of it. That's why they hang about here. So the guy did have a tumour?'

'Lift it up a little…one the size of a corn cob! He died all of a sudden, up near Porto. I only ever saw him here once. Such a fuss over a house he never even saw finished. Like they say: "Nest done, man undone!"'

'It'll be the heirs who get to enjoy it now. Probably a bunch of money-grubbers, eh Senhor João?'

'From what I hear, they're his nephews. You can let go of that now.'

'Life's made for folk with uncles.'

The door swings on its hinges with a sigh. Perfect. The master carpenter wipes his nose and adjusts his wire-framed spectacles, which have a chip in one lens.

'It's a law of life. No one gets to stick around.'

He studies his work, gives the door a swing and, as if he were addressing it, repeats:

'No one gets to stick around.'

'The house seems to be jinxed, Senhor João. That man put all his hard-won earnings into this plot of ground and…'

'Hard-won or not, now he'll be making do with four boards and six foot underground, same as the rest of us. Just think, this place was meant to be ready by October. It won't even be done by New Year!'

'Not even by Carnival, Senhor João. But if the old fellow hadn't kicked the bucket, his nephews would have had to wait a very long time…'

Meanwhile, the house is heaving with activity. The stonemasons and bricklayers are busy with the monumental staircase. Others are laying the geometric mosaic in the entrance hall, leading to steps of the finest black marble streaked with white, decorated with plinths and columns, above it the ceiling skylight made of stained glass showing cornucopias of flowers and fruit. The lobby and main staircase will be bathed in a gorgeous, gentle light from above. However, for the time being, grubby old scaffolding planks mask the noble proportions of the house's architecture and block the glorious light from on high.

The contractor carries on running up and down its three storeys like a madman, yelling, slipping, spitting out black saliva and curses. Hurry, hurry! There's a constant banging of hammers, increasing in pace and noise. Outside in the enclosure, pulleys groan as they hoist blocks of marble. Plastering trowels nervously scrape the walls. The owners are in a hurry. As ever, they arrive in two cars early in the morning to cast a critical eye over everything, making new plans, passing new judgements. The job still isn't getting done! They want to move in by New Year, invite guests to a party, just a small one naturally, since they would still be in mourning… But it's all in such a state! Yet to come are the decorators and gardeners, carpets and furniture, not to mention the chandeliers—*the chandeliers!* All still to come. Not a chance it'll be ready within the month!

'Not even for Carnival!'

That explains the foreman's bad temper, as he grinds the cheroot stub between his teeth, and hops over the railings to where the joiners are laying the parquet flooring.

The foreman nervously checks his watch; it's already gone eleven-thirty! Mornings go by in a flash, no one knows how, and the work appears to be at a standstill. Yet nobody pauses, smokes, or chats (he looks around in the hope of catching someone out), nobody goes out to answer a call of nature or fetch a cup of water from the pump. The workmen listen in silence to the contractor's yelling, feel the foreman's watchful eye on them, as sharp and piercing as the point of a file.

Everyone is rushing except for the dead man who now has a house of his own, built—naturally enough—in the Manueline style, up in Agramonte, complete with an altar table and cedars planted in amphorae at the entrance. All of that, however, is nothing compared to the quantity of materials consumed by this place. It is a bottomless abyss. The contractor predicts its ruin, as the racket of activity increases and the building works vibrate, hum, and sing in the workers' hands.

The contractor has vanished out the back, into a kitchen that shines like a hospital ward, with its marble walls and floors, porcelain fittings and tiles and white metal pipes. Nothing is missing. They are in the process of installing the central heating boiler. As to the dead man, he no longer has either light or warmth. Tough luck!

All of a sudden an unusual, strange, and brutal sound permeates the house, stifling the noise of work and the foreman's voice, freezing the hurried movements of the men: a plank has groaned and snapped somewhere, then more planks creak, nails squeak as they part company with their sockets—a hoarse cry followed by a chorus of hoarse cries of shock and terror—then a clatter of planks and rafters that come spinning down, banging and crashing into each other as they do; a bulky, dull thud and then an instant, no more than an instant, of frozen silence, white and empty...

Some of the workmen run for the exits, thinking of an earthquake, destruction, flight:

'The house! The house!'

In the kitchen, the contractor blanches, tears the cheroot from between clenched teeth:

'What's going on? What's going on?'

'The scaffolding! By the staircase! Help!...'

A rapid trampling, a confusion of feet, and echoing cries which suddenly seem to rattle the solid concrete of the whole house. From all sides—the outside enclosure, the terrace, even the cellar—men come running ashen-faced, stammering, trembling, questioning, mesmerized by the creaking planks and the cries rising from the grand hall. You couldn't tell they had been scattered through the whole house just moments ago; now all gathered together in an influx of shock and terror, they appear in a mass, a multitude. Cries and yet more cries...The contractor arrives, his colour livid, heart pounding, elbowing his way through the men, mouth gaping:

'What is it? What is it? Let me through!'

They could hear groaning. The sound of groaning cutting through the chorus of voices, the wall of men assembled there, pushing and shoving to get a view. A thick cloud of dust rose and now clouds every detail and feature. The house appears deserted, with no sign of activity. All the men are there.

Part of the scaffolding around the staircase has collapsed: suspended mid-air, hanging from a bent nail by a tie, a thread of nothing, beams teeter ominously. Panic-stricken, the workmen have scampered all the way down like monkeys. One man, just one, of all those who had been working up there under the skylight fell right from the top—tangling in the planks, clinging onto a wood beam—to the bottom. There he lay motionless, curled and contorted. From the pile of dusty rags and twisted limbs issue a moan and a trickle of blood, just one.

His eyes are closed, and more moans emerge from between clenched teeth. He has landed on the fine sawdust intended to protect the mosaic marble flooring. ('Let's hope it doesn't leave a stain,' thinks the contractor.) A dark stream of blood seeps from one ear. The contractor pushes the men aside and approaches, his face now flushed and heavy under the grizzly grey beard. Another silence. All eyes are fixed on him. Then, suddenly, ten or fifteen pairs of scrawny hands emerge, extended to lift the injured man. Everyone starts talking at once, in a confused babble no one listens to or understands. The foreman fails to appear. The contractor passes his hand over his eyes and feels the sweat on his jowls.

Then looks up: he sees the menacing beams dangling from way up high; the disjointed scaffolding; his face a mask of fear. Still no one pays him any attention

'Call a car—or a taxi!'

'There are trucks on-site, lads...'

'A doctor! Someone get a doctor...'

'You go and find one.'

(Everyone knows who 'you' is: the next man along.)

'Call the police... We need a proper stretcher!'

The wounded man's teeth are chattering, he is seized by convulsions. A couple of the men reverently disentangle his limbs, which the fall has left lying in painfully grotesque positions.

'It was from right up at the top...'

'For three days the scaffolding has been...'

'Who is he?' the contractor asks in a low voice, pondering the consequences.

'Pedro, it's Joaquim Pedro!'

'He lives over in Pote d'Agua.'

The men are shoving, shouting, gesticulating, running, powerless and bewildered, tripping over like startled ants.

'Run! Get a taxi... to the hospital!'

Only João, the master carpenter, keeps calm. He's seen it all in his time. He wipes the sweat from his brow. Then puts his spectacles on again, grabs hold of an apprentice and yells into his ear, to rouse him from his state of immobilized panic.

'Go out onto the road, boy... grab the first car you see!' and he gives him a push.

The youngster, wearing patched overalls, jumps over a window sill and flies down the road, splashing through the mud. Workmen are scattered throughout the other construction sites in the new neighbourhood, oblivious as they carry on mixing concrete, hammering beams, building walls, laying tiles.

Moments later, a blue taxi pulls up at the metal gates the colour of living flesh, to receive its first customer from the opulent new house. Six pallid, silent workmates carry out the injured man laid out on a litter made out of boards. A rattle comes from his mouth and his whole body shakes violently between convulsions.

'Grab him at that end.'

'Open the door!'

'From the other side... Lay his hand down! That's right.'

The driver peeks out, and jumps up from his seat to lend a hand.

'Was he attacked?'

'No, the scaffolding...'

The body ends up doubled over on the back seat.

The line of dark blood trickles from his ear, soaking into his striped shirt and worn overalls.

'Careful with my upholstery!' grumbles the driver, who wouldn't dare refuse to take an injured man, a fellow worker. 'Blood makes a real mess of plush.'

'You go with him, lad,' the old man tells the electrician. 'Look after him properly!'

Twenty heads turn to look once more at him.

'You go with him too, lad,' the old man orders the carpenter. 'And come right back, understand?'

The boy, looking solemn and determined, sits down next to the driver. In order to close the rear door they are obliged to push inside a foot that persisted in sticking out, wracked with spasms, still in its muddy boot laced with twine.

The taxi revs up. Blue petrol fumes emerge...

'Now we're off!'

The workmen remain on the pavement watching them leave, before filing back indoors, head bowed, dragging their feet. They have little to say.

'He won't be coming back, that one.'

'No way. He's already more dead than alive. His bones are bent all out of shape!'

'His insides are all crushed. I saw him land head first on the sawdust: *bam!* I'm surprised his brains didn't fly right out!'

'Did you see? His mouth was all full of blood. He won't be coming back.'

'It's the luck of this house!'

'The contractor knew only too well how the scaffolding...'

'I told him about it three days ago. He paid no attention, of course...'

They move off slowly. What now? The hesitant protest dissipates through the house. The men become dispersed again, each to their own task, from the enclosed terrace. Those who can, go back to work. The plasterer's trowel smooths a wall like a caress. Heavy hammering rings out from the parquet.

The contractor has left in another car, either for the hospital or to see his lawyer. Minutes tick by. Until the foreman's shrill whistle flies through the house. Master João, the carpenter, checks his old pocket watch, shakes his head, and sniffs:

'Today of all days, you've sounded it punctually! You time-thief, you're always five or ten minutes late... What's got into you?'

The morning rain has eased off, and broad beams of tepid sunlight are shining on the yard, where rain-washed blocks of white stone now shine. The men file out down the back stairs in their torn, faded shirts, with their lunch boxes under their arms, but no one feels hungry. They can't obliterate the image of the crunched body, crumpled and trembling, the trickling blood, the foot boldly sticking out. Some wash their hands under the water jet coming from the pump. They break up into groups around the yard.

The last man to emerge is the master carpenter. His door has finally been hung to perfection. He puts his spectacles back in their case, places them in his pocket, blows his nose loudly and philosophically, before heading down the long corridor towards the service entrance. On reaching the outside stairwell he descends three steps before pausing. The bright façades of the surrounding new, bourgeois neighbourhood are tranquilly drying out in the December sun. Masses of eucalyptus, pine, and olive trees are sharply outlined in the background, beyond which lie more shiny new houses. The scenery is tightly enclosed in the midday silence. Master João enjoys nature, trees, and the earth, and no break in the working day passes without him casting a tender look at the picture before his eyes. He inhales a deep breath of fresh air. It was here that at some other time... when might that have been?... in the days of Heliodorus, Magellan, Gneco the sculptor... Life was different then, with different joy, different faith... People nowadays... He lowers his eyes: over there is the gate through which that poor man was carried, only just before.

Extraordinary that not a trace should remain. Death arrives and nothing changes!

No, not everything has stayed the same...

Senhor João, the master carpenter, blinks: oh Hell! The old woman is propped up against the wall! They had all forgotten her. There she is, just like every other day, modest and motionless, her umbrella clutched to her chest, her eyes fixed to the ground, waiting for her son, his lunch in her basket growing colder. 'Now what do we do?' the carpenter mutters to himself. He looks around for help. Nobody around. He doesn't dare either to go further down the staircase—she knows who he is—nor to go back up. He stays stock still, anxious, still sniffing, and blinks at her again. What can he say to her? How can he say it? Master João has seen a good many things in his life: men killed at work, or in the war in Africa, or under the hooves of the horses of the National Guard, when they were out on the street calling 'Long live liberty!' But something such as this! How was he supposed to tell the old woman that her son, her support...?

From behind the house where the noonday sun is blazing, the workmen's voices can be heard indistinctly. They are bound to be discussing the accident. And if she overhears what they're saying, learns what has happened? The carpenter is growing apprehensive. He doesn't want her to be caught unprepared! The best is to act bravely, go straight up to her, and say something to forewarn her. At this the old woman, clearly already concerned at her son's late arrival, perhaps already aware of being anxiously watched, turns her head and her eyes meet those of the carpenter. Their looks remain locked for a moment, many metres apart, but Master João can't bear the weight of her troubled and weary expression and his legs start to tremble under him. He glances away and clears his throat in embarrassment. Oh Hell!

At the top of the road a vehicle has just stopped on the main street: within moments someone descends, before the tram quickly resumes its rapid journey. A boy in blue overalls: it's the young apprentice, now running over to them. He can be seen behind the fence. The carpenter feels a surge of hope. Even at this distance, the boy has spotted him, and runs faster, gesticulating, calling out something...

'Master João! Master João the carpenter!'

'What is it? What?'

The old man realizes what's happening. He bounds down the staircase, runs across the corner of the yard separating him from the gate, passes in front of the old woman who follows him with her eyes, then heads along the pavement as fast as his legs can carry him, to head off the apprentice:

'Shut your mouth, lad. Shut that mouth of yours! The old woman his mother is here. Doesn't know a thing as yet. So what happened...?'

'He... he...' the boy stammers, grabbing the old man's arm. But his tears well up, drowning his words.

'He what? What did he?' Master João shakes him impatiently. 'He what? Talk! He died? Come on, out with it. Don't cry, lad! Did he die or didn't he?'

'It happened on the way there... he was gasping... a mass of blood came out of his mouth... by the time we arrived he was dead. The electrician stayed there with him. His overalls were all covered in blood... They were going to open up his stomach, poor fellow!'

They have reached the gate. The old woman might hear them... The carpenter lowers his voice and tells the boy:

'Dry your eyes, it'll be all right. Now go round the back and come in by the front gate. They're having lunch around on the other side of it. That way the old woman won't see you. Go, go and tell your workmates. I'll see you there shortly... Give me strength!'

The carpenter takes a deep breath. Reluctantly he walks through the gate and goes over to the old woman, who makes an indecisive gesture, without letting go of her umbrella.

'So you're still there, ma'am? Waiting for your boy? He's not here at the moment. He went out. He might be gone a while. It'd be best for you to head for home. It may well be that he doesn't make it back to work today. He might, but again he might not.'

The old woman observes him with growing anxiety in her glittering eyes.

'Nothing important, no need to torment yourself with. He got a whack on the arm... It'll turn out to be nothing. It occurred there on the staircase, a scratch on his arm. They took him to San José hospital.'

While she listens, her hands nervously clutching her umbrella, the old woman is going white: only her nose reddens, and appears to grow larger; her eyes, hazy and inflamed, like two glowing embers coated in ash. Her toothless mouth hangs half-open exposing a cork-dry tongue. She frowns and champs on her bare gums and her dry, purpled lips—you would think she were chewing over the words she was hearing. She pauses a while like this, before she can manage to stammer:

'Please tell me, Master João: you say my son was taken to hospital? In that case he's dead. My son is dead! Tell me, Master João: is he dead? Is he?'

The workmen, who now know all about it from the apprentice, are coming over in a group, silently and hesitantly, from the other side of the yard, without daring to draw close to the two old people.

'What do you mean *dead*, ma'am? I told you he received a whack. And that's no reason at all for...'

The old woman shakes her head obstinately:

'My son is dead. Senhor Master Carpenter. You're a kind man and don't wish to tell me the truth. See!' the old woman points to the workers gathered at a distance. 'They're all staring at me! Oh!'

The master carpenter feels his tongue tying itself in knots, rejecting an outright lie. Silence envelops the house with its deserted scaffolding, and all the building works across the neighbourhood, during the lunch break. Further on, in Sete Rios, a train whistles loudly as it passes, wrapped in a thick cloud of white steam. Master João looks at his waiting workmates, who have left him there on his own to discuss death with an old woman while tears blur his vision. ('How many years has it been since I cried?')

'Is he dead, Master João? Tell me the truth, by the five wounds of Our Lord Jesus Christ! Oh my son, is he no longer of this world?...'

The old woman raises her hands in supplication, lifting the umbrella on high like a crucifix. By now, the carpenter can no longer see anything through his tears but a form-less black mass. Far better to have had the earth open and swallow him up! But at long last his fellow workers are drawing closer, even beginning to form a ring around them. Now it's possible to observe how skinny the old lady is. You could almost think she was about to cry and scream, as her skinny ankles give way so that she collapses onto the mud and cobbles; but not one tear falls from her rheumy red eyes. Her dry half-open mouth has no scream to offer. She puts the umbrella in her basket, and with her arthritic hands re-arranges her lock of hair and mantilla. Her hazy eyes suddenly seem to be gazing into the distance. The whole of her trembles like a blade of grass, as she masticates incoherent words that only the carpenter can manage to catch:

'The life of the poor. The life of the poor. One today, tomorrow another... Only the old woman remains. She's still here. The old woman. Thanks be to God!'

She picks up her basket, her umbrella and, more stooped than ever, turns her back and leaves, hopping across the puddles, over the mud. Arriving at the gate she stops, turns back, lifts up the umbrella like a crucifix and says, in a clear voice they can all hear, a voice that seems to emerge from another body or another world:

'Do you understand what I am saying to you? That God our Saviour helps those who give work to the poor!'

They watch her depart, stumbling and zigzagging down the wide new road gently caressed by the sun. The carpenter's eyes feel like a pair of embers. He turns to the men, standing stock still... He has to find something to say to them. At that moment the foreman's whistle can be heard, recalling them to work. The master carpenter loses control, raises his clenched fists, and yells:

'Murderer! Murderer!'

A man appears at a ground floor window with a whistle in his mouth; he looks like a chirping sparrow. There's an instant of expectation, then suddenly the apprentice picks up a stone and flings it. There follows a hail of sticks, stones, and rubble flying through the air, splitting door frames, breaking through window panes, ricocheting off walls and rebounding off the drawing room parquet, hitting the man in the face and on the head, so that he flees, his hands covered in the blood pouring from his cuts. A voice rings out clearly across the yard:

'Everybody out, lads! From today, none of us picks up another tool!'

Next day two or three unknown men, out of uniform, idly take a turn around the avenue and the near-deserted streets, where they read newspapers, seated on some nearby steps. The owners arrive early, grumble about delays in the construction, and threaten to take the contractor to court. The man provides explanations while chewing on his cheroot and shrugging his shoulders. The foreman has disappeared. The workmen turn up reluctantly and late, gathering around the master carpenter who reads them these sobering lines from page six of the morning paper:

> *In a house under construction in Palhavão, bricklayer Joaquim Pedro fell from the scaffolding. Taken to the San José Hospital, he was pronounced dead on arrival and delivered to the Mortuary. The unfortunate man leaves no children.*

Not a word about the old woman. Nor about the protest or the letter the builders had sent to the newspaper.

The master carpenter crumples it up.

What is to be done? Slowly, work resumes. The contractor (who didn't dare to sack anyone) has reverted to pacing up and down wearing his trousers rolled, a stubble beard and an anxious expression, the perpetually extinguished half-cheroot clamped in his jaw. The scaffolding is back in place over the grand staircase—with the same rotten, worm-eaten boards and the same squeaky nails. And the prayer *Lord God please help those who give work to the poor.* Once more the men work on in silence. The insatiable house of the rich continues to expand. Joaquim Pedro is in the morgue, the base of his skull cracked like a clay pot, over which so many doctors engage in study of the effects of Fate. The house has to be ready by the New Year. Hurry, hurry. The furniture, decoration, guests...

'This house goes beyond that, it is jinxed,' announces the painter, Luis. 'You wouldn't catch me living here, not even for free. Not if they gave it to me!'

Time rushes by, hands start working faster, until the whistle sounds. This time it's the contractor who blows it. The whistle goes and men jump down from the scaffolding and the ladders, drop their tools, and head out into the yard. The sun is shining, the wind has moved round to the northeast, the weather is getting cooler.

And that's when they see her coming: hopping over the mud, her mantilla still in position, the umbrella clasped to her chest, and the baskets in her right hand. She's in a hurry—the whistle has already sounded, and I'm still over here! She enters the gate, stumbles across the rubble-strewn yard, and props herself up against the wall in her usual position. She sets down the basket, holds her hands to her chest, and fixes her eyes to the ground.

There she remains. The men move off in pity, almost in apprehension. Madness beckons like a door open on the world of maggots. Only the master carpenter, old like her and who has seen many things in his time, permits himself to stare at her. With difficulty, he swallows a piece of fried fish and some dry bread. He cannot tear his eyes away from the crazy and crumpled old woman and shakes his head.

'Go home, my dear. Don't risk catching a cold out here.'

But she doesn't say a word. She gives him a questioning look, mute and non-judgemental. Her nose and lips are red with cold.

When the contractor blows his whistle again, the old woman rearranges her mantilla over the lock of hair, picks up the basket and departs, hopping along on her skinny ankles.

From that day onward she returns every day, just when the whistle blows. Perfectly punctual! Her son has been under the ground for a long while now, but she never misses a day. She opens the basket, sits herself down on her cloth spread out on a stone, and looks straight ahead as if her son were there before her. Sometimes she speaks but nobody knows what they say to one another, the old woman and the ghost of her son, the bricklayer.

Afterwards, when the whistle calls the men back in, she puts her bowl and clean plates back in her basket, adjusts the mantilla around her neck, and departs down the same path, hopping over the mud and puddles in order not to dirty the shoes that must have all of ten years' wear in them, as well as being relics from the time of her late beloved son.

The Whistler

Mário Dionísio

It became very difficult to move freely at that time of day. Shops, offices, and workshops were ejecting hundreds of people onto the streets. Streets, squares, and tram stops, designed at a time when there weren't as many people in the shops, offices, and workshops, filled up from one moment to the next. Even the city centre's spacious squares resembled narrow corridors where people were forced to bump into one another. Upright citizens found it temporarily necessary to set aside their manners, with no remedy other than to join in the pushing, shoving, and intermittent cursing. Trams were huddled along the track, rammed front to back. They progressed sluggishly, crammed to the limit inside and out, with hundreds of passengers filling every corner of the tramcars, spilling onto the running boards, even out onto the open-air platform, all piling out of shops, workshops, and offices. What made it busier still was that, on a fine day like this, streets in the Baixa were full of fashionable people, enjoying their five-o'clock stroll, meandering into boutiques and tea houses as a way to kill time and see familiar faces, only returning home for dinner.

Such a multitude made fraternization obligatory. You were forced to apologize to the errand boy whose foot had just been trodden on, implore passengers hanging off the tram to squeeze in a bit further so you could get a toe-hold—nothing more than a toehold—on a tiny corner of the running board, and you were often required to smile at complete strangers. Fashionable men and women found all this extremely tiresome. Worst of all was the unavoidable imperative to travel on crowded front and rear tramcar platforms, no longer occupied solely by gentlemen, but also by vulgar little men and women who gave off an unbearable smell. Yet what else could you do besides throw yourself into a sea of people who pushed, thrusted, stamped, and wrestled? What could you do besides join in with the pushing, thrusting, stamping, and wrestling yourself?

The tram trundled slowly onwards, as packed as all the rest. Happily, there were still a few well-mannered men left in the city, a few little women who still remembered their place. It was only thanks to them that the few respectable ladies and gentleman, some of them obliged to forfeit shoes and hats in lunging forward with the hordes, were able to obtain seats.

During the first minutes of the journey the passengers shifted uncomfortably in their seats. Those left standing attempted a few steps inside the tramcar to see if there was any hope of finding an empty seat. You could overhear complaints on the outside platforms. Eventually, everyone somehow settled in, squeezing up against each other, lifting up their arms to liberate their purchases above the crush, and checking that the coats and bags in which they carried their money were safely secured. Then the conductor yanked the bell, repeatedly and impatiently, and the tram moved off in silence. The respectable gentlemen began to unfold the evening papers they had just purchased and scan the news. The ladies nervously straightened their hats and their coat collars. They fished little mirrors out of their bags and looked themselves over: their hats, their hair, their eyes, their lips. It was incredible: one had been left with her hat skewed completely to one side, another had lost a glove in the confusion. Then they would stow the mirrors back in their bags, shift into a more comfortable position, and discreetly brush their fingers over the rings on each hand to check they were still in place. Then they glanced at around at the other passengers blankly, as if not really taking notice of anything. The respectability which had evaporated during the traumatic experience of boarding the tramcar was quickly recovered.

On every corner, the wheels screeched in their grooves under so much weight. Otherwise, the silence was only broken by the bell, the rustle of newspapers, and the voices of passengers travelling on the front platform, audible when the door opened for someone to get off or when the wary conductor came in to check if anyone had dared to board without a ticket.

Everything had returned to normality: the steady progress of the tram, the respectful distance between passengers, the payment of fares. So it proceeded sluggishly forwards, around corners or on the straight, through streets and squares.

At a certain point, however, a loud commotion could be heard coming from the rear platform. It sounded like angry protests. Heads turned inside the car.

A man was pushing his way through the crush, forcing his way onto the tram. He demanded to be let through, claiming there were still empty seats at the front. They told him there weren't any seats, that he couldn't get on, and not to be so rough. He pushed so hard that he squeezed himself on. He squeezed so much that he was able to reach the middle of the tramcar. He continued to advance, before taking an empty seat next to a corpulent lady in a corner on the last row of the car. There resulted a shocked, collective silence. Nobody had noticed that space. What a smart operator! Fortune clearly does favour the bold.

The man was wearing a shabby cap and a brown over-coat, shiny in patches, its collar turned up. He must still have been young, but his hair was flecked with grey and he hadn't shaved. He didn't so much sit as bury himself down in the seat, his hands thrust deep into his pockets. A strange fellow. The woman next to him furrowed her brow and tried to shift up still further. But this only encouraged him to settle in more comfortably although her intention had been to make him aware of how much his behaviour was inconveniencing her. But the man didn't interpret it like that, or at least affected not to. He looked vaguely at the passengers in front of him and began to whistle. A carefree whistle right there inside the carriage. At first, it was a very low, almost imperceptible whistle. Then, little by little, he grew more animated. The whistle became more intense. You could hear it the length of the whole tram. The passengers, who had recovered their composure, pre-tended not to be bothered by either the man or his whistle. And they were relieved at the sight of the conductor mak-ing his way towards the new arrival. He was bound to tell the man to be quiet. But the conductor did nothing of the sort. With the wad of tickets in one hand and wielding a well-sharpened ticket punch, he confined himself to enquiring: 'Mister?' The passenger took his hand out of his pocket and, whistling all the while, extended his upturned palm turned, with a single coin on it. He received his ticket and shoved his hand back down inside his pocket. Everybody was observing the scene with curiosity. But as soon as the man returned their look, they averted their eyes, as if he weren't really there after all.

Sometimes the whistle was low. At others it was high, with modulations. Nobody knew what that tune was, least of all the man himself. It was just something in the air, with no beginning or end. He was content for it to come out just the way it did. Sometimes he would repeat sounds, like a refrain. At others, most of the time in fact, he would move on to fresh harmonies, either softly or emphatically, without the slightest reference to what had come before.

Passengers had begun to exchange furtive glances. They had never seen anything like this before. One or two of the gentlemen raised their eyes from their newspapers to glare at the man in the shabby cap and brown overcoat, in the vain hope that he might be shamed into reconsidering his position and stop whistling. The large woman next to him stared in astonishment. She'd never witnessed anything like it.

The silence inside the car seemed to amplify the whistle's volume. The passengers couldn't help thinking that it was rather a pleasant sound. It was simply that a tram wasn't the place for such a performance. Why didn't the conductor intervene? Inside the carriage, the conductor represented authority. Why didn't he say something to him? The conductor was being too indulgent towards the little man. The truth was there was no regulation to prevent people from whistling on the tram. There were notices prohibiting smoking and spitting inside the car, stuck to the windows which were to remain shut in winter. But there wasn't a single word about whistling.

Suddenly, a small child seated beside a window, who had grown tired of peering out at the street and counting how many street lamps were lit and how many were not, took an interest in the man. Wasn't he funny? She found the little man ever so amusing with his shabby cap, his brown overcoat, and his whistle. She was a tiny little girl, slightly pale, and dressed all in blue. She became so fascinated that she began to clap her hands in delight. But a pretty young woman sitting beside her shot her a disapproving look. Gently, she took hold of the girl's hands and pulled them apart, as if to make a point. She should sit there and stay quiet and subdued. It was very bad manners to make a noise on the tram. A good little girl never attracts attention. 'What have I always told you, darling?' However, it wasn't long before the woman, who really was very young herself, forgot her own manners for a few seconds. She began to listen to the man's whistling, her eyes staring down at her knees. She stared past the beautifully wrapped packages in her lap without seeing them. What would happen if she couldn't contain herself any longer and began whistling too? Deep down, she admired the carefree attitude of the man in the shabby cap. Wouldn't it be charming if she, a married woman and mother of a five-year-old girl, began whistling on trams whenever the fancy took her? When she was her daughter's age, the pretty young woman had often gone to the countryside dressed in old clothes so she could throw herself down on the grass without a care in the world. She had had a smooth, fresh-sounding voice that wouldn't startle a dove. Kind-hearted women friends used to pick her up and toss her into the air. And she would laugh, laugh, laugh until she ran out of breath.

Once in a while, someone would ring the tram bell and then descend. Little by little, the tramcar emptied. And, little by little, the remaining passengers grew used to the whistle. Some could no longer hold back their laughter. Had anyone ever seen anything like it? They pursed their lips to maintain their composure. The corpulent woman sitting beside the man was finding it particularly difficult to contain herself. Her features contorted. Her eyes were shining with strange intensity. She was making such an effort not to laugh, it almost induced tears. Indeed, her eyes were shining with unnatural brilliance. She couldn't carry on. Her reaction was understandable: sitting next to him, she couldn't help catching the eye of all the other passengers. It was contagious.

The pretty young woman was thinking about fresh air and her childhood, which felt a very long time ago. At school she had learned how to whistle and spin tops. There were voices which had been buried deep inside of her: 'Do good little girls whistle, Nini?'

A moment later, never for an instant pausing in his whistling, the man stood up and rang the bell. He was a modest little man, with a shabby cap, a brown overcoat and greying hair. But he radiated a visible disdain for everyone on the tram. All eyes were fixed on him. With disdain? With irony? Or with envy? He opened then closed the door after himself without a backward look, and jumped down from the tram.

The passengers could no longer control themselves. They exchanged glances and surrendered themselves to laughter. A wave of pure pleasure rippled through them. The child who had clapped her hands wiped the condensation from the window and followed the man with her gaze. She watched him cross the street and head off along the pavement, hugging the houses. The whistle faded further and further into the distance until, finally, it disappeared completely. It was then that the girl's mother opened her eyes. Nobody called her Nini anymore. Nini was her daughter's name. These days she was the one who said: 'Do good little girls whistle, Nini? Good little girls never make a noise!'

There was a faint smile upon the lips of each of the passengers in the car. They all somehow appeared younger and more attractive. It wasn't long, however, before their smile began to fade. The passengers became conscious of their momentary lapse of composure. The smile slowly came apart. How pathetic. They had no other word for their behaviour: yes, what utter nonsense. The gentlemen once again ducked behind their newspapers. The ladies fiddled with their coat collars. The child went back to counting how many of the street lamps were lit and how many were not.

Everything returned to a ponderous and dignified silence.

The Fiancé

Agustina Bessa-Luís

He didn't know when he would see her again. Her voice was still ringing in his ears, filled with the cooing of a tender tyranny, a gentleness that was perhaps no more than surprise at the obsessive exhilaration of his love. She kept her feelings well-guarded, even to the point of meanness. But it was clear she had been greatly shocked by the revelation of his poverty and it had weakened her resolve: what she had once regarded in him as repellant now appeared romantic. For her, pity was the only possible expression of love. So it was they became engaged.

Once again, parting after one of those brief days of bliss when the heart appears to exist as if suspended between two poles of time, he had told her, 'Your hair is the colour of dead leaves.' The lime trees rippled above their heads, tramps yawned on slatted benches, the city extended its countless branches, bristling with trams and telegraph wires, domes and chimneys. Little whirlwinds of swirling dust reached the treetops where leaves were falling, filtering the static, russet light. So the day had gone by. But it was only much later that he parted from her, waving to him from the landing as if over the railing of a ship; she leaned on the marble staircase and wept, finding something approaching a respite in her tears, almost a reason for becoming the target of his own affections. He smiled up at her imploringly, struck dumb, his expression anguished. He was, no more than an adolescent, almost emaciated, his large eyes looking as if they had been outlined with fine brush-strokes, resembling the painted face on an Egyptian sarcophagus.

He didn't live in the city, and for him each visit meant a regime of privation, calculation, rationing, financial chance, as only someone who is poor and has the experience of a serious dearth of money can imagine. Each meeting with his fiancée was preceded by sleepless nights, absorbed in pondering deeply over the means to acquire the minimum sum necessary. Each loving sigh was paid in toil, ingenuity, and incalculable energy. What for others was no more than an easily transferable fancy, a manifestation of bourgeois sentiments, a natural consummation, a misfortune, a joke, a footnote, a bout of colic, or a distraction, for him amounted to the decisive victory in a battle, a reason for being, the historic expression of his humanity.

Now he was making his descent into the city centre, heading, to shorten the journey, down semi-hidden, poorly lit backstreets he barely recognized. It was a cold night; halos around the streetlamps formed impressionistic blotches upon walls bathed in a greyish-blue light. The paving slabs ran with sticky humidity where you could expect to find swirls of algae and rotting sludge exuding from the drains. The town was silent and lifeless in this quarter, where the buildings, with their projecting balconies, resembled old stage sets.

The fiancé continued at his purposeful and almost aggressive pace, so typical of timid young men. Occasionally a window display would cause him to stop and shiver. He was wracked with hunger; an insidious, treacherous, merciless hunger; the hunger of perennial fasting, more terrible than utter starvation, because it erodes, because it tempts, because it remembers. He knew that the spectacle of those windows filled with provisions—the grey-skinned pigeon lathered in glaze, the suckling pig whose pink fibres were like the inside of an oyster and possessed the greasy sheen of mother-of-pearl, towers of pastries, fish or fruit— would provoke in him a covetous yearning were he to stop and stare. So he passed by without turning his head, maintaining an expression full of concentration and severity. From doorways, pale silhouettes of women called out to him in desperate and brutal voices, with mock-discretion, cynical apathy, exhaustion, optimism, promises or insults. He could distinguish forms moving towards him, hems of dresses dragging along the ground; shining in the darkness he could descry unusual arrangements of glass beads, hands grazed him in passing, dustings of rice-powder, so dense they made him cough, reaching his nostrils along with the rank odour of rags, of cheap lotions perfumed with artificial jasmine. He carried on, affecting calm. He had the impression of stumbling, of making a vain effort to move forward, while his feet refused to obey him; that the women, submerged in burrows from where their soft gloating voices could be distinguished, observing him, laughing amongst themselves, and rolling their eyes. He visualized them as seductive, every last one. Some, with yet strong yet neglected bodies, resembled over-ripe goddesses, wearing tired and candid expressions, for whom nudity is no more than a natural state, and immorality nothing more than habit and custom, just another way to affect morality. Others—acid, sharp as daggers, possessing every intuition born of vice, capable of high spirits because they so rarely succumbed to sentimentality—held for him the hint of a conquest, all the more intense and tempting because with them it was difficult to imagine yourself lord and master. Nonetheless, he passed them by without looking back.

He was reaching the city centre, stirring now with a quiet and ghostly hum. The pavements, the asphalt on the roads, and the black and white stonework pedestrian areas, all emitted a pale waxy glow. At tables outside cafés couples lingered, stirring their drinks with the resentful and oppressive tedium of those who have grown bored in each other's company. The fiancé paused, looking at a young man who, leaning over a discarded newspaper, was regarding the completed crossword with a perplexed expression. 'Ah', he thought, 'he should be my friend.' He was tempted to approach him, perhaps to begin one of those warm and pointless conversations that contain the secret of masculine communication. However, he abstained from doing so. Now he was heading away from the centre, to the area behind the station where dubious boarding houses were located, installed in old buildings whose windows were like arrow-slits draped in ragged curtains stained with decay. He knocked at one, and was answered from within by a clatter of feet coming down the stairs. A man with a fringe of grizzled hair over his eyes, cautiously cracked open the door.

'Ah! It's you!' said the man, but didn't immediately recognize him. He was wearing a loose-collared, dirty cotton nightshirt and seemed barely half awake. 'There's an empty bed on the first floor.'

'I need a room to myself.'

'Fine!' And the man shrugged his shoulders. He yawned and blinked his eyes, as if in a daze, but was, in spite of everything, courteous and patient, welcoming and good-natured. Which is why the youth preferred this hostel. When he took his seat before the steaming dish of baked cod set among tepid stalks of cabbage, their leaves pinned back like snippets of oilcloth, he felt no sense of shyness, humiliation, or any of the painful complexes that often arise from misery. The man would sit next to him, happily devouring one plateful after another, asking questions and listening with rapt attention as if to Marco Polo himself, newly returned from Cathay.

But the cordiality he displayed was as altruistic as it was superficial. It is in this kind of brief and fortuitous contact between men that we discover the greatest fervour to communicate, the greatest heart, the greatest desire for companionship and mutual support. Faced with someone that we suspect we may never see again, who will soon be lost in the swirl of the world, and to whom, therefore, we are not chained by the fastidious duties of a long-term relationship, we instantly devote a kind of gratitude which translates into expansive camaraderie, openness, and generosity which, too often, we may go a whole lifetime without experiencing towards another being who shares our blood and lives under the same roof. Man is terrified of emotional imprisonment; therefore, strangers become his dearest friends.

'Go on up', said the proprietor. 'There's a room in the garret. Goodnight!'

The man followed him up, leaning heavily on the banister, which wobbled. Large black cockroaches scuttled along the skirting board, startled by the light. The man threw out insults at them, but in an indulgent tone of voice, and without bothering to chase them away. On the second floor, he stopped.

'Goodnight! It isn't much of a room', he said, by way of farewell. But the young man didn't hear him. He continued climbing, breathing heavily, because the staircase was interminable and virtually perpendicular. He found the room, separated from the landing by a curtain which felt like worn sackcloth to the touch. It had a tall window that reached the ceiling and, even when lying prostrate on the bed, he could see the cityscape, the trams with their faintly gleaming tops, neighbourhoods with their backstreets of hovels roofed with corrugated iron, dilapidated awnings, advertisements daubed on walls. Such a peaceful view seemed to the youth like an unexpected luxury, some kind of reward. Such is the relativity of compensation. Like the monk who opens the door to his cell and closes it once a chill sets in, simply to have some semblance of warmth, the young man revelled in the pathetic spectacle of the sleeping town, glimpsed from the pallet roughly set down between two dirty panels, from where his horizon was blocked by a wall on which travellers' clumsy fists had scratched their debts, and drunken sailors had scrawled the names of women, ports, and vessels. He thought of his fiancée. She had a faint chickenpox scar at the corner of her mouth, like the dimple of a perpetual smile. He smiled too, thinking about his fiancée, and didn't notice that the pallet reeked and that the sheets gave off a putrid odour of human bodies, marked by poverty with the stigma of living decomposition, more odious than even disease or death. He fell asleep immediately, breathing softly, his closed fist resting on his chest. The cold rose up and enveloped him like an icy glacier. Frost slid down the window panes in large drops, and inside the room everything seemed to have become petrified, frozen, and fragile as if beneath a magic spell. Belfries rang out the hour, and the greenish light of dawn gradually began to seep and spread, as if suppurating in the gloom. The damp and hanging mists dispersed, mingling tones of grey and frosty silver, the spectral shades of dawn. The young man awoke, raised himself up on his elbow, and peered out at the dense vapours rising like columns of smoke from a crater. Buildings loomed as if bearing the weight of the surrounding shadows, resembling giants suspended over the abyss. Poor neighbourhoods were like hunchbacked gnomes, contorted and steeply sloping, with vigorous, threatening yet bruised limbs. Graphite domes and towers emerged, shiny and frivolous. There were tiny sparkles in the glint of a glass tile, sedimented frost in the eaves, ephemeral glimmers, inconsequential and almost illusory. The shrill, persistent chirping of a flock of birds filled the air, and a ruffling of feathers could be heard emanating from pigeons making their nests in the nooks between caryatids and stone facades, in church roofs and stone monuments. The fiancé murmured: 'Today is the day I must depart once more.' And his heart heaved with a sorrowful resentment, as if he were admonishing the ingratitude of another. He opened the window, shaped like a high, pointed arch. A small railing, reaching to his knees, was all that separated him from the abyss, from the still shadowy labyrinth of streets, ringing with early morning street cries. He could see shunting engines, their smoke hovering above the station platform nearby, sounding their whistles, emitting puffs of steam, and hear the constant din of pistons. He would have to leave soon, he thought. A great coldness enveloped him. The room behind him was bare, abhorrent, and cold; and he became momentarily aware of a stirring in all those other lairs that belonged to beasts stretching themselves, with foul and filthy yawns, the rank breath of thousands of mouths contorted into grimaces of lethargy and slumber, an instant in which he sensed, experienced, and lived the rhythm of that entire great cage of a city, with its houses, alleyways, truckle beds, green park benches, *boudoirs*, cinemas, bureaucracy, brothels, newspaper offices, and the four-poster beds in bourgeois homes. The whole impression of senile somnolence, stagnation, hypnotic fatalism, penetrated him for a moment, establishing itself within his spirit like a revelation. The city, a robust organism prostrated at his feet, injected with opiates and brought to ruin, terrified him. 'Ah', he said to himself, 'how like a kingdom of shadows this looks, and how melancholy.' And he laughed. He felt as though his heart were replete. There was nowhere left inside him for any concern beyond his love; he was rendered incapable of experiencing any lasting emotion, neither pity, anger, nor fear, so exalted did he feel by his love, projecting itself and radiating along every nerve, inhabiting his understanding of time and truth. Up there, from the heights of that narrow skylight, he looked down upon the city, which seemed to shudder to its foundations as early-morning trams sullenly set off down their tracks along the streets. It was as if all the towers dangled from his fingertips like Christmas decorations, so much did his inner being channel a magnificent power, a kind of terrible sorcery which sprang from his nerves and rained down in space, over the world and life, over all desire, all creation. 'All of this is mine! The world and the heavens are mine!' he exclaimed, and he shivered, overwhelmed with emotion. He was excited by a strange sense of power. Was this the day he must depart? No matter, he would be back, nothing could stop him returning. What were these petty demands, obstacles, rejections, betrayals, pitfalls, all these snares in which life entangled him? Where did they come from? Was it from each of these miniscule and restless beings thronging far below his feet, a twisting, turning, swarming antheap, a vague and disoriented commotion? He laughed again, leaning out over the abyss. Money? He would have it. Victory? It would be his. He extended his arm, and could touch the pinnacles; he could warm the palm of his hand on the face of the sun; he would reach for the horizon and use a finger to trace the diameter of the earth itself. By way of weapon—invincible, unyielding, implacable—he was possessed of passion. If every man down below, moving through the current of the city, sighing and cursing under the weight of his burden, only knew the imperative power of the will engaged in surrendering his passion, even unto hell itself, then he would attain within him a human yet irresistible divinity. Doomed love affairs are both the executioners and redeemers of this world. Above all, they are perhaps the reminiscence of a divine state that man aspires to reclaim.

'I don't care that I must depart', said the fiancé, filled with a bold and haughty violence. All around him there was misery and desolation. Pale rays of daybreak poured over the rooftops, illuminating ugliness and ruin. Only the light was beautiful, resplendent with rainbow tinctures, golden threads, and clusters of stars sparkling between.

Walking in Lisbon

José Saramago

Here is the collar. The traveller made a promise and now he keeps it: as soon as he gets to Lisbon, he will go to the Archaeological Museum and look for the collar worn by the slave owned by the Lafetá family. On it can be read the following words: 'This negro belongs to Agostinho Lafetá do Carvalhal do Óbidos.' The traveller is repeating it again here in order to impress it on forgetful memories. If a price were put on this object, it would be worth millions upon millions: as much as the monastery of the Jeronomites next door, as much as the tower of Belém, as the presidential palace, as all the cars put together in one huge traffic jam, probably as much as the entire city of Lisbon. This collar is just that, a collar that hung round the neck of a man, soaked by his sweat, and perhaps also some drops of blood from a lash of the whip aimed at the back but which missed its target. The traveller is truly grateful to whoever picked it up and did not destroy the evidence of such a horrendous crime. Since he has never refrained from speaking his mind, however outlandish his views may have seemed, he will now make another judgment: that the collar of Agostinho de Lafetá's black slave should be placed in a room all of its own, so that there will be nothing to distract visitors from it, and no one could say they had not seen it.

The Archaeological Museum has many thousands of exhibits that the traveller will not mention. Each of them has its own history, from the Palaeolithic age to the nineteenth century, and they all have something to teach us. The traveller can imagine starting with the earliest and going down through history to the most recent. Apart from a few well-known gods and Roman emperors, the rest are unknown, faceless and nameless. Every object has its description, and the traveller discovers to his astonishment that when it comes down to it, the history of mankind is the history of these objects and the words used to name them, the links between words and objects, their use and subsequent neglect, how, why, where, and by whom they were made. Envisaged like this, history does not become cluttered with names, it is the history of material acts, of the thoughts that shaped them and the way they shaped thoughts. For example, it would be good to take one's time to find out about this bronze goat or that anthropomorphic plate, this frieze or that chariot dug up in Óbidos, so near to Carvalhal, in order to show that it is both possible and necessary to relate one thing to another in order to understand each.

The traveller regains the street and feels lost. Where should he go now? What is he to visit? What shall he leave aside, either on purpose or because of the impossibility of seeing and commenting on everything? And anyway, what does it mean to see everything? It would be just as valid to stroll through the gardens and to go and look at the ships on the river as to visit the Hieronymite monastery. Or do none of this, but simply sit on the bench, even on the grass, enjoying the splendid bright sunshine. It's said that a ship at anchor is not sailing. That is true, but it is preparing to set sail. So the traveller fills his lungs with fresh air, like someone hoisting sail to catch the sea breeze, and sets course for the monastery.

He is right to choose naval imagery. Here to the left of the entrance is a statue to Vasco da Gama, who discovered the route to India, and on the right the reclining figure of Luís de Camões, who found the route to Portugal. Nobody knows where his bones lie; those of Vasco da Gama may or may not be in the monastery. There are genuine bones to be found far at the back on the right, in a chapel off the transept: here lie the mortal remains (or do they?) of Dom Sebastião, the unhappy sixteenth King of Portugal. But that is enough of tombs: this monastery of the Hieronymites is not a cemetery, but an architectural miracle.

The architects of the Manueline period produced a great deal. They never made anything more perfect than the vault of the nave here, anything more daring than the transept. The traveller feels overwhelmed. He has so often defended the beauty of unadorned stone, but now he surrenders to the decorative detail of what looks like weightless lacework, and before pillars that seem too slender to support any weight. And he recognizes the stroke of genius in the decision to leave part of each pillar free of any decoration. The architect, reflects the traveller, desired to pay homage to the basic simplicity of stone, while at the same time introducing a feature that would give the spectator a jolt, waking him out of his lazy way of looking.

But what captivates the traveller most of all is the sight of the vault over the transept. Twenty-five metres high above a floor twenty-nine by nineteen metres. The vaulting soars in a single arch, with no pillar or column to support it. Like the hull of a giant ship turned upside down, this soaring belly shows its ribs, its innermost structure, so amazing the traveller he does not know whether he should kneel on the spot and praise whoever conceived and designed this miracle. He walks down the nave once again, and again is overcome at the sight of the slender shafts of the pillars which, high above him, embrace or sprout the ribs of the vaulting like palm trees. He wanders up and down in the midst of tourists speaking half the world's languages, while a wedding is taking place. The priest is pronouncing the customary fine words, and everybody looks happy: let's hope they go on being so, and have all the children they may wish for, so long as they do not forget to instruct them to enjoy the beauty of these vaults, which their parents have hardly glanced at.

The cloister is very beautiful, but it does not impress the traveller, who has very firm views in these matters. He acknowledges its beauty, but he finds its decorative detail excessive, overloaded; beneath this ornamental surface, however, he can sense the harmony of its structure, the balance of the great blocks of stone, strong yet light. Nevertheless, it fails to excite him. His heart has gone out to other cloisters he has seen. This one offers pleasure only to his eyes.

The traveller has not mentioned the portals: the one facing south that gives on to the river; the other to the west on the church's axis. They are both beautiful, carved like filigree, but although the first is more elaborate because it extends over the whole front, the traveller prefers the other, possibly due to the magnificent statues of King Dom Manuel and Queen Dona María, by the sculptor Chanterenne, but more probably because of the harmony it achieves between Gothic and Renaissance features, without any Manueline effects. Perhaps in the end it is simply the traveller's known preference for simpler, more rigorous forms. Other people have other tastes, and so much the better for both.

Between visiting the Maritime Museum and the Museum of Carriages, between maritime and land means of transport, the traveller decides first to visit the tower of Belém. At a moment when coining rhymes was easy, and patriotic feeling hard, a poet wrote: 'Só isto fazemos bem, torres de Belém' ('There's only one thing we do well, build towers of Belém'). The traveller does not agree. He has seen enough to know there are many other things at which the the Portuguese excel, like making those vaults in the monastery of the Hieronymites he has just emerged from. Either the poet Carlos Queirós did not see them, or else he simply preferred the easier rhyme with Belém to the harder one with monastery. However, that may be, the traveller cannot understand what military use this exquisite piece of jewellery could have been put to, with its wonderful lookout turrets facing the River Tagus, much better suited to watching naval regattas than for positioning cannon to help repel an invader. It should be said that the tower was never used in any battle. Luckily for us. Imagine what destruction this lacework of stone would have suffered in some sixteenth-century bombardment or military attack. As it is, the traveller can visit the rooms on each level, go up to the lookout posts, lean over the battlements facing the river, and still feel disappointed he cannot see himself looking out from such a beautiful spot. And finally he can go down to the dungeons where the prisoners were kept. It must be one of man's strange obsessions that he cannot see a dark, dank place without wanting to imprison a fellow human being in it.

The traveller did not spend much time in the Maritime Museum, and even less in the Museum of Carriages. To see ships out of water makes him sad, to see carriages used for pomp and ceremony annoys him. The ships, thank heaven, can at least be taken back to the river and shown in their element, but what a ridiculous sight it would be if one of the carriages were to set out creaking its way along streets or motorways, like a clumsy tortoise that would lose its legs and shell along the way.

For several good reasons and an even better one (to clear the cobwebs from his mind) the traveller next went to visit the Museum of Popular Art. It's a respite from the heat. It also raises any number of questions. The traveller would prefer to divide it in two, each part capable of considerable development: popular art as such, and the art of work. This does not mean making two separate museums, but making the links between art and work more visible, showing the compatibility between the artistic and the useful, between object and sensory pleasure. This is not to deny that the museum offers an extraordinary lesson in the beauty of objects, but museums suffer from the original sin of a simple exhibition of things which have far from simple ideological implications, such as those behind their creation and organization. The traveller enjoys museums, and would never vote for their abolition in the name of so-called modern ideas, but nor can he accept that they offer simply a neutral catalogue, taking an object, defining it, and putting it in among other objects, thereby severing the umbilical cord which connected it to its creator and its users. A popular ex-voto has to be put in its own social, ethical, and religious setting: equally, a garden rake does not make sense without reference to the task it was made for. New moral values and technology are pushing these objects into the realms of archaeology, and this is just one more instance of the increasing demands made on museums.

The traveller spoke of any number of questions being raised. Here is just one of them: seeing that Portuguese society is undergoing such a crisis of taste (especially with regard to architecture and sculpture, objects in everyday use, and in urban planning) it would be no bad thing if those who are producing and pronouncing judgment over this general aesthetic decline, as well as the few who are still struggling against this suffocating trend, were to come and spend a few afternoons in the Museum of Popular Art, simply to look and think, to try to understand this almost vanished world and discover what part of it can be rescued to pass on to the future in order to safeguard our cultural survival.

The traveller walks along the river, so different here to the tiny stream in its upper reaches near Almourol, but still almost a trickle compared to the wide estuary it becomes at Sacavern, casts a contented glance at the bridge now named after the 25 April* and climbs the steps of the Rocha do Conde de Óbidos to visit the National Gallery. Before going in, he enjoys looking at the ships at anchor, the intricate confusion of hulls and masts, funnels and winches, the booms and pennants, and promises himself to return at night to marvel at all their lights and try to discover the meaning of the metallic sounds echoing sharply over the dark water. The traveller wishes he could have twenty senses, but accepts he still would not find them adequate, so contents himself with the five he was born with to hear what he sees, see what he hears, to smell what he feels with his fingertips, and taste on his tongue the salt which at this very moment he can hear and see on

* 1974, the date of the Carnation Revolution that ended 48 years of military dictatorship under President Oliveira Salazar. It has since come to be celebrated as 'Freedom Day'.

the wave sweeping in from afar. From the height of the Rocha do Conde de Óbidos, the traveller applauds life.

For him, the most beautiful picture in the world is in Siena in Italy. It is a tiny landscape by Ambrosio Lorenzetti, scarcely larger than the palm of a hand. But the traveller does not wish to be exclusive in these matters: he knows full well there are other pictures which could claim to be just as beautiful. The Portuguese National Gallery houses one of them: the panels displaying the *Life of St. Vincent of Fora*, besides those of the *Temptations of St. Anthony*. Then again there is *The Martyrdom of St Sebastian* by Gregório Lópes. Or the *Descent from the Cross* by Bernardo Martorell. Every visitor has the right to choose, select his own most beautiful painting in the world, the picture which at a certain time and in a certain place he puts above all others. This museum, which should be called by the more evocative name of the Museum das Janelas Verdes* after the street where it stands, is not particularly well known or well endowed compared to rivals elsewhere in Europe. But if properly exploited, there is more than enough in it to satisfy the aesthetic requirements of all Lisbon and its surroundings. Without entering the adventures into which the rooms devoted to foreign paintings could lead the visitor,

---

* *Street of Green Windows*, most likely named after the typical dark green shutters that line the street, including the whitewashed former palace that now houses the museum.

the traveller found himself delighting in the ways that the sixteenth-century rooms of Portuguese works of art dealt with human and animal figures, the landscape, still lives, real or imaginary architecture, natural or skilfully altered flora, ordinary or ceremonial dress, and all those pictures which delve into fantasy or copy foreign models.

And, to go back to the panels—whether or nor they are by Nuno Gonçalves—they show every feature of what makes up our Portuguese character. Depicted in the background of the portraits, these versions are so powerful they cannot be diminished by the greater emphasis placed on the figures of kings, nobles, and clerics in front of them. It is not hard to match these faces to contemporary ones: in the country outside the museum there is no lack of twins to those shown here. But beyond the easy exercises in nationalism these juxtapositions offer, here in Portugal we seem incapable of drawing any more meaningful conclusions about our national identity. At a certain point in our history, we Portuguese lost the ability to recognize ourselves in the mirror these panels offer us. Obviously, the traveller is not referring to the cult of the age of discovery for which these panels provided inspiration. Rather, he places these paintings alongside the objects he saw in the Museum of Popular Art, and hopes this will explain his train of thought.

We are not talking about the Louvre in Paris, the National Gallery in London, the Uffizi in Florence, the

Vatican, the Prado in Madrid, or the Gallery in Dresden. But this is the Museum of the Janelas Verdes: this is what we have, and it is good. The traveller is a regular visitor; he has the healthy habit of visiting one room at a time and then leaving. It's a method he recommends. A meal of thirty dishes does not nourish thirty times more than a meal of just one dish; looking at a hundred pictures can destroy the benefit and pleasure one of them might give. Apart from the organization of space, arithmetic has little to do with art.

The weather in Lisbon is fine. The road leads us down to the garden of Santos-o-Velho, where a clumsy statue to Ramalho Ortigão is swallowed up in all the greenery. The river is hidden behind a line of sheds, but its presence can be felt. And beyond Cais do Sodré it spreads out to embrace the open space of the Terreiro do Paço. This is a beautiful square we have never quite known what to do with. There are few government offices or dependencies left here: these huge blocks from the time of the Marqués de Pombal do not fit in with today's view of a bureaucratic paradise. As for the square itself, at times a vast car park, at others a lunar desert, what it needs is shade, shelters, focal points that could attract people to meet and talk. It is a royal square: one king was assassinated in a corner here, but the people have never taken to it, except in short-lived moments of political passion. The Terreiro do Paço still belongs to King Dom José. The statue of one of the dullest monarchs ever to reign in Portugal faces out over a river he must never have liked and which is far greater than he ever was.

The traveller walks down one of the commercial streets with a shop in every doorway and banks which are shops as well. He tries to imagine what Lisbon would have been like here without the earthquake. What was lost from an urban point of view? What was gained? A historic town centre was lost, and another gained, which with the passage of time has also become historical. There is no point arguing with earthquakes, or trying to ascertain the colour of the cow whose milk was spilt, but as the traveller ruminates, he comes to the conclusion that the reconstruction of the city ordered by the Marquês de Pombal did represent a huge cultural break from which the city has not yet recovered, and which continued in the confused waves of architecture that have washed over the urban space since then. The traveller is not nostalgic for mediaeval houses or Manueline revivals. He simply notes that these and other reconstructions were made possible only due to the violent shock of the earthquake. Not only houses and churches collapsed. A cultural bond between the city and its inhabitants was also broken.

Rossio Square has fared rather better. It's an important thoroughfare, and has a lot of traffic, but for this very reason it detains the passer-by. The traveller buys a carnation from one of the florists by the fountain, turns his back on the theatre they refused to name after Almeida Garrett, then pursues the ups and downs of the Rua da Madalena to reach the cathedral. Along the way he is frightened by the cyclopean equestrian statue to King João I in the Plaza da Figueira. This is a perfect example of the sculptural problem we have only rarely been capable of solving: there is usually too much horse and too little man. Back in the Terreiro do Paço, the sculptor Machado de Castro showed how it should be done, but few others understood him.

The cathedral almost succumbed to the changes made following the earthquake, in the seventeenth and eighteenth centuries, all of which were thoughtless and in bad taste. Luckily the front was restored and now looks dignified with its military-style crenellations. It is not by any means the most beautiful church in Portugal, but that adjective can be applied without hesitation to the magnificent combination of the ambulatory and the chapels of the apse, whose equal would be hard to find. The French Gothic-style chapel by Bartolomeu Joanes is also noteworthy. We should mention too the harmonious arches of the triforium, on which the eye lingers. And if the visitor has a romantic soul, there is also the tomb of the unknown princess, which will guarantee a tear. The sarcophagi of Lopo Fernandes Pacheco and his second wife, María Villalobos, are similarly fine works of art.

Until now the traveller has not mentioned the fortress named after St George. Seen from here below, it is almost concealed by vegetation. A fortress during so many such distant battles, from the time of the Romans, the Visigoths, and the Moors, it now looks more like a public park. The traveller doubts whether this is an improvement. He recalls the grandeur of the impressive ruins at Marialva and Monsanto, and cannot help feeling that here, despite the restorations which were intended to strengthen the sense of the fortress's military heritage, the strutting white peacock or the swan on the lake makes more of an impression. The terrace makes one forget the fortress. It does not seem possible that the knight Martim Moniz should have been crushed to death keeping this gate open during the recapture of Lisbon.* That's how it always is: one man's death is another man's garden.

The traveller has not shown any great affection for eighteenth-century Portuguese art, whose chief manifestation

---

* According to the legend, Martim Moniz was a knight participating in the Christian invasion force, led by king Afonso I of Portugal, in the Siege of Lisbon, during the Reconquest. At one point in the siege of São Jorge Castle, he saw the Moors closing the castle doors. He led an attack on the doors, and sacrificed himself by lodging his own body in the doorway, preventing the defenders from fully closing the door. This heroic act allowed time for his fellow soldiers to arrive and secure the door, leading to the eventual capture of the castle. Martim Moniz was killed in the incident. In his honour, the entrance was dubbed *Porta de Martim Moniz* (Martim Moniz Gateway). There are currently several monuments and parks named after Martim Moniz in Lisbon. One of Lisbon's metro stations is named after him. The station features a stylized graphic depiction of the event on its walls.

is the so-called Joanine* style, rich in carvings and Italian imports, as displayed at Mafra. Unless it is some obscure form of flattery, it seems somewhat lacking in imagination to call these styles after kings and queens who never so much as lifted a finger to help: the British have their Elizabethan or their Victorian styles, we have our Manueline and Joanine. This just shows that the people, or those who claim to speak on their behalf, still cannot do without a father or mother, however dubious the paternity may be in cases like these. But then the monarchs had the authority and the power to dispense the people's money, and it is thanks to this obsession with paternity that we have to congratulate Dom João V for building the church of Menino-Deus in gratitude for the birth of an heir to the throne. The floor plan of the church is attributed to the architect João Antunes, who was no slouch if this magnificent building is anything to go by. The Italianate style could not be avoided, but it does not manage to obscure the flavour of our native soil, as can be seen from the use of tiles. With its octagonal nave, the church forms a perfect balance. When he has time, the traveller must find out why the church was given the unusual name of the Child Jesus: he suspects this was decided by His Majesty, who subliminally linked the dedication of

---

* King João V ruled from 1706 to 1750, and during his reign many Baroque architectural projects were undertaken, such as the monastery at Mafra and parts of Coimbra University. Many of Portugal's Baroque churches date from this period, with splendidly gilded interiors.

the church to the son and heir born to him. That is just the kind of thing that Dom João V would do, given his well-known *folie de grandeur*.

It is not yet time for the traveller to go down to the Alfama. First, he will visit the church and monastery of San Vicente de Fora which, tradition has it, were built on the site of the camp the German and Flemish crusaders put up when they gave the first Portuguese king, Dom Afonso Henriques, a vital hand in the taking of Lisbon. Nothing remains of the monastery the king had built on this spot: it was demolished at the time of Philip II and replaced by the one still standing. It is an impressive architectonic machine characterized by a certain frigidity of design that is typical of Mannerism. The façade, however, shows a distinct if subdued personality of its own. The interior is vast, rich in mosaics and marble, and with an imposing altar commissioned by Dom João V that has heavy pillars and large saintly images. What must not be missed in San Vicente de Fora are the tiled panels in the entrance, especially those which represent the conquest of Lisbon and of Santarém, conventional in their distribution of figures, but full of movement. Other tiled panels decorate the cloisters. In its entirety, the church gives a cold impression, monastic in the sense given by the eighteenth century and which has defined it ever since. The traveller does not deny that there is merit in San Vicente de Fora, yet he does not feel a single fibre of his body or soul truly moved by it. This may be his fault, or simply perhaps because he is moved by other, stronger sensations.

Now it's time for the traveller to visit the Alfama, accepting he will be lost by the second corner, and determined not to ask for directions. This is the best way to get to know the neighbourhood. There is a risk of missing some of the famous places (the house in the Rua dos Cegos, the house of the Menino de Deus, or the one in the Largo Rodrigues de Freiras, or the Calçadinha de São Miguel or the Rua da Regueira, the Seco das Cruzes, etc.) but if he walks far enough, he will eventually see them all, and in the meantime he will have discovered a thousand and one surprises.

Alfama is a mythological beast. It is a pretext for all kinds of sentimentalism, something everyone lays claim to for their own advantage. It does not shut itself off from any visitor, but the traveller can feel the ironic glances shot at him. *These are not the serious, closed faces of Barredo.* Alfama is more than accustomed to cosmopolitan life; it plays along if it thinks it can get something out of it, but in the secrecy of its narrow houses there is much mirth at the expense of anyone who thinks he can know it after spending an evening there, attracted by the Feast of St. Anthony, or its delicious rice dishes. The traveller follows the winding alleys, almost brushing his shoulders against the houses on either side while, up above, the sky is a chink of blue between overhanging roofs barely a foot apart; he crosses sloping squares where the different levels are accommodated by two or three flights of steps: he can see there is no shortage of flowers in the windows, or canaries in their cages, but the stench from the open gutters in the streets must be even stronger inside the houses, some of which have never seen the sun, and others at street level whose only window is the open front door. The traveller has seen much of the world and of life, and has never felt comfortable in the role of a tourist who goes somewhere, takes a look at it, thinks he understands it, takes photos of it, and returns to his own country boasting that he knows the Alfama. This traveller must be honest. He went to the Alfama, but he does not know what it is. All the same, he walks and walks, and when he finally comes out at the Lugo de Chafariz de Dentro—after being lost more than once, as he knew he would be—he wants to immerse himself once more in its dark alleys, twisting dead-end streets, slippery flights of steps, until he feels he has at least learnt the first few words of the immense dialogue taking place between houses and inhabitants, involving personal histories, laughter, and the inevitable tears. Transformed into a mythological beast by outsiders, the Alfama lives out its own, difficult story. At times it is a healthy beast; at others it cowers in a corner licking unhealed wounds that centuries of poverty have incised in its flesh. Even so, these houses have roots, unlike many other slums.

Beyond it is the Military Museum, with its bounty of glory, flags, and cannon. It is a place to look at with a clear mind and sharp awareness, in order to try to detect the civilian spirit that seeps into everything, the polished bronze, the steel of the bayonets, the silk of the standards, and the stiff cloth of the uniforms. The traveller has another of his very original ideas: anything civilian can become military, but it is very hard for anything military to become civilian. So many misunderstandings are rooted in this lack of reversibility. And such roots are dangerous.

This part of the city is not beautiful by any means. The traveller does not include the river in this judgment, because however much it is obscured by ugly sheds, it always finds a ray of sunshine to catch and return to the sky. But the buildings, the old ones like walls perforated by windows, and the new ones like something out of a neurotic dream, are horrendous. The traveller takes heart in the promise of the convent of Madre de Deus.

Seen from outside, it is a huge wall with a Manueline portal at the top of half a dozen steps. It helps to know that this doorway is fake. It is a curious case of art imitating art in an attempt to recover reality, none too concerned whether it was reality that the imitated art has imitated. This sounds like a puzzle or a tongue-twister, but it's true.

When in 1872 it was decided to reconstruct the old Manueline façade of the convent, the architect studied the *Retábulo de Santa Auta* in the National Gallery and copied line for line from the painting—extending them only a little—the details of the portal through which the procession carrying the relic entered. João María Nepomuceno considered this idea as brilliant as that of Columbus' egg, and perhaps it was. After all, in order to rebuild Warsaw following the devastation of the Second World War, they copied the eighteenth-century paintings by the Venetian artist Bernardo Bellotto, who spent some time in the city. Nepomuceno came before him, and he would have been silly not to make use of the documentary evidence at hand. Yet we would all look silly if it transpired that the original portal was not like the present one at all.

Despite the fact that the decorative elements of the church, the choir, and the sacristy date from different periods (from the sixteenth to the eighteenth centuries), the impression given is one of a great unity of style. This unity probably derives in part from the golden splendour everything is coated with, but it would be more honest and preferable to say it is the result of the high artistic value of the entire building. The brightness of the light, which leaves no relief untouched, nor any colour dull, is part and parcel of the feeling of euphoria the visitor experiences. The traveller, who has always protested so strongly at excesses of gilt carvings that can stifle the architecture, finds himself overwhelmed by the rocaille of the sacristy, one of the most perfect examples of a certain kind of religious sentiment, precisely the kind known in Portuguese as 'a spirit of the sacristy'. No matter how many pious images cover the walls, it is the sensual appeal of the world that shines out from the mouldings and the altarpieces, with all their shells, feathers, palms, scrolls, garlands, and festoons of flowers. To express the divine, all this is covered in gold, but it is life outside that swells through this decoration.

The main choir is a jewel casket, a reliquary. To express the inexpressible, the sculptor used every stylistic resource. The visitor loses himself in the profusion of forms; he renounces using his eyes as an analytical tool and contents himself with the overall impression, which is not so much a synthesis as a bewilderment of the senses. The traveller wishes to sit in the stalls to recover the simple sensation of plain wood, something that has survived all the carver's modelling.

The cloisters and the adjacent rooms house the Museu do Azulejo.* It is worth mentioning that the exhibits are only a very small part of all those kept in store awaiting the space and the money to display them. Even so, this museum is a precious place that the visitor regrets is so

* The [Painted] Tile Museum.

little visited, or if it is visited, is so poorly made use of by those responsible for design in our own day. As far as Portuguese decorative tiles go, there is a lot to be done, not in the sense of rehabilitation, but of understanding. Understanding what it means to be Portuguese because, whereas for a long time this century they were an undervalued art form, now tiles have made a strong comeback for the external facing of buildings. To unfortunate effect, in most cases. Those who design these modern tiles do not know anything about them. And to judge by the evidence, those who teach about tiles or write about them are pretty ignorant too.

The traveller retraces his steps, discovering another fountain called El-Rei, although no one can be sure which king is meant because it was partly built during the reign of Dom Afonso II but in the reign of Dom João V it acquired nine spouts, all of which are now dry. It is most likely that its name comes from Dom João V the Magnanimous, a great one for naming things. There is little else left of the old city in these parts: only the Casa dos Bicos, a poor cousin of the Palace of Diamonds in Ferrara, before the beautiful Manueline portico of the church of Conceição Velha, which the earthquake did not succeed in toppling.

Walking beneath the arcades of the Terreiro do Paço, the traveller thinks how easy it would be to breathe life into these archways by organizing small fairs on particular days each week or month, for the sale or exchange of stamps or coins, or exhibitions of paintings and drawings, or to set up flower stalls; with a bit of thought there are plenty of things it could be used for. Then this sandless, duneless desert would be repopulated. The people who rebuilt Lisbon bequeathed us this square. Either they knew in advance we would need it as a car park or they were trusting to our imagination, which, as is plain for all to see, is negligible. Perhaps the fact is that the motorcar has taken the place reserved for imagination.

The traveller has heard that somewhere down this street there is a Museum of Contemporary Art. As a man of good faith, he believed what he heard, but as someone who also believes in objective truth, he has to confess he does not think he saw it. It is not that the museum lacks merit, because some of the pieces are quite interesting, but the promised contemporaneity must have been from some other age, before even the traveller's time. The paintings by Columbano are excellent, and if other names do not immediately spring to mind, it is not to belittle them, but to indicate that either the museum does what it says it is meant to, or merely adds to the confusion over our national artistic heritage. The traveller is not worried about critics and artists in general, because they obviously know who and what they are, but about the general public, who must come in here at a loss, and leave completely lost.

In order to rest and recuperate from the museum, the traveller climbs up to the Bairro Alto. Anyone with nothing better to do stirs up rivalries between this district and the Alfama. That is a waste of time. Even at the risk of exaggeration, which always accompanies making any peremptory judgment, the traveller considers them radically different. It is not a question of saying that the one or the other is better, which would only lead to the problem of what is meant by better in this kind of comparison, but simply that the Alfama and the Bairro Alto are diametrically opposed, in their appearance, their language, in their ways of being on a street or leaning out of a window, in a certain highhandedness of the Alfama which in the Bairro Alto becomes insolence. And my apologies to anyone living there who is not in the least bit insolent.

The church of San Roque is close by. To judge by its appearance, we wouldn't rate it very highly. Inside it is a sumptuous hall where in the traveller's modest opinion it must be hard to talk to God of poverty. Look for example at the St John the Baptist chapel which the inevitable Dom João V commissioned from Italy. It is a jewel of jasper and bronze, mosaics and marble, totally inappropriate for the passionate forerunner of Christ who preached in the desert, ate locusts, and baptized Jesus with water from the river. But after all, time passes, tastes change, and Dom João V had a lot of money to spend, as we can tell from the reply he gave when told that a carillon of bells for Mafra would cost the astronomical sum of four hundred thousand *reis*: 'I didn't think it was so cheap, I'll have two of them.' The church of San Roque is a place where one can find a saint for every occasion: it is crammed with relics, and has images of almost the entire celestial host in the two exuberant reliquaries flanking the high altar. But the saints did not smile down on the traveller. Perhaps in their time such things were seen as heresy. They are wrong: nowadays looking kindly on someone else is a way of attempting to understand them.

Lisbon never liked ruins. They have always been either rebuilt or pulled down altogether to make room for more lucrative buildings. The church of the Carmo is an exception. In its essence, the church is as the earthquake left it. There was talk at one time of either restoring or rebuilding it. Queen Dona María I was keen that it should be rebuilt, but her plans came to nothing, either due to lack of money or lack of real interest. So much the better. But the church, dedicated by Nuno Álvares Pereira to Our Lady of Victories, had to suffer numerous indignities after the earthquake: first it was used as a cemetery, then a public rubbish dump, and finally as stables for the City Guard. Even though he himself was a horseman, Nuno Álvares must have turned in his grave as he heard the horses neighing and kicking, let alone when they took care of more basic animal needs.

Today finally the ruins are an archaeological museum. It does not have many exhibits, but they are of considerable historical and artistic interest. The traveller admires the Visigoth pilaster, the Renaissance tomb of Rui de Meneses, and other objects he will not detail. It's a museum that pleases for many reasons, to which the traveller will merely add one other of his own: he enjoyed it because it showed how the stone was worked, the traces of man's hand. There are others who obviously think the same way, and this gives the traveller the pleasant feeling of being accompanied: in two engravings from 1745 by Guilherme Debrie, one of the façade of the convent, and the other a side view, naturally the figure of Nuno Álvares Pereira appears, conversing in courtly fashion with nobles and clergy, but so too does that of the stonemason, cutting the stone blocks, with the rule and square he used to help build this and other convents.

The traveller's trip round Lisbon is coming to an end. He saw a lot, but hardly saw anything. He wanted to take a good long look, but perhaps hasn't succeeded. That is the risk one always takes on a journey. He walks up the Avenida da Liberdade, a fine name that should be preserved and defended, walks round the gigantic pedestal supporting the statue to the Marquês de Pombal and a lion, symbol of power and strength, although there is more than one malicious tongue which suggests that this is a case of taming the beast of popular power, so that it lies at the feet of the strong man, and roars to order. The traveller likes the Parque Eduardo VII (although here is a place name which, meaning no disrespect to Great Britain, we could surely change to something closer to our own interests) but regrets it is like the Terreiro do Paçó, an abandoned empty space scorched by a hot wind. He visits the Calouste Gulbenkian Museum, which without doubt represents a prime example of how to use the science of museums to present a non-specialized collection that offers a documented view of the evolution of the history of art.

The traveller is leaving Lisbon by the bridge over the Tagus. He is heading south. He sees the tall columns, the giant arches of the Aqueduto das Águas Livres over the River Alcântara, and reflects on how long and desperate Lisboan thirst must have been. Their need for water was assuaged by Claudio Gorgel do Amaral, the administrator of the city who started the project, and the architects Manuel da Maia and Custódio José Vieira. Probably to satisfy Dom João V's Italianate taste, the first person in charge, although only for a short time, was António Canevari. But those who really built the aqueduct and paid for it with their own money were the people of Lisbon. This was recognized in the Latin inscription on a plaque on the arch in the Rua das Amoreiras, which read: 'In 1748, in the reign of the pious and magnanimous King

João V, the senate and people of Lisbon, at the people's expense and to their great satisfaction, brought the Águas Livres into the city after a wait of two hundred years, thanks to twenty years' hard work in drilling and transporting blocks of stone up to a distance of nine thousand yards.' This was nothing more than the truth, and even the proud Dom João V could not deny it.

Nevertheless, only twenty-five years later, by order of the Marquês de Pombal, the inscription was deliberately altered 'in order to obliterate the existence of the previous inscription'. And in place of the truth, the hand of authority imposed deceit and lies, robbing the people of all their effort. The new plaque, approved by the Marquês, falsified history in the following way: 'In the reign of Dom João V, the best of kings, the benefactor of Portugal, safe and healthy water supplies were brought to the city of Lisbon along aqueducts strong enough to last forever, and measuring nine thousand yards in length, the work being carried out at reasonable public expense and with the sincere gratitude of everyone. In the year of Our Lord 1748.' Everything was falsified, even the date. The traveller is convinced it was the weight of this plaque which finally precipitated Sebastião José de Carvalho e Melo into hell.

Cais do Sodré Station

Orlanda Amarílis

'I honestly didn't recognize you.'

Andresa rummages in her memory to locate recognizable family traits in the face of the woman now sitting in front of her. She looks as if she belonged to nhô Teofe's people. Was it that he was originally from São Nicolau, nicknamed Benjamin Franklin by his students? Or might she be a relative of Faia's brother nhô António Pitra, who long ago set sail for Argentina?

Oh dear, whenever she meets people such as this woman, newly arrived from their distressed and grieving lands, she can almost always connect them to one family or another. If she has never met them personally, well, she's sure to know their father, a brother, or maybe an elderly aunt, renowned for her home-made confectionery. Perhaps even one of the servants from the old house. A conversation like ours grows from an initial connection, extending into something gentle and pleasant.

'I was looking at you, you know, because I could tell straight away that you were from back home', continues Andresa, gazing with a smile at the scrawny figure sitting next to her.

The woman smiles back. A shy, tranquil smile.

Encouraged, Andresa ventures another question:

'Have you been here very long?'

'Yes, going on two months now. Not too long, but it's something.'

Andresa adjusts the handbag on her lap, distractedly fingers its miniature tortoiseshell clasp, uncertain as to why she had undertaken a conversation with this woman. Does she know her? How? Where from? Not really, not unless from way back in the days of drinking herb tea. I really am a scatterbrain.

Would I be Andresa Silva, Andresa, daughter of nhô Toi Silva from Casa Madeira?

Yes ma'am, that's me, nh'Ana's niece, nhô Toi's daughter. That's right.

What else is there to talk about? One day I'll kick this habit: the need to lend an ear to every busybody from back home. I don't care who I bump into next, I don't know them. Quite enough of all this nonsense.

Her fingernails trace the outline of the tortoiseshell clasp and her reflection is lost in the black sheen of her patent leather handbag.

'Well, and if it wasn't for Papa's illness would I be here? Oh heavens, no. Whatever for?'

Andresa blinks and surprises herself with her reaction.

Is that really you, Andresa? Is that you carrying on this insipid conversation? You could have avoided it, but conversations are like that. They have a thread, a line to follow. So don't seem so surprised you took the risk.

'Ah! Is your father sick?'

'Papa is dead.'

And, with a sigh, her voice dies away as well.

'I'm sorry, I didn't know', Andresa commiserates.

The woman digs a handkerchief out of her bag and blows her nose. Then she replaces the handkerchief, closes the bag, and sits staring at the toes of her shoes.

'He didn't want to leave, even when his life depended on it. When Dr. Santos told him that he needed to see a specialist, urging him to take the next boat, my Lord did he kick up a fuss. He wasn't going to come, he was *not* going to come! In the end, he assumed an aggrieved air and began waging war on the household. He talked on and on, banging his clenched fist on the table, warning us all: No one bossed *him* around, he was still the master of his own mind. We had a hard time trying to convince him. He said other things too. He argued and argued until he ended up collapsing in his deckchair. I can still see him, head slumped forward, hands dropped on his lap. Occasionally he'd wake up, raise his head and open his eyes, only to snap them shut and continue snoozing. All in order to carry on fishing for moray? How pitiful! He must have been dreaming.' She pauses for breath. 'He used to say: if I ever do make the leap over to Lisbon, I'm going to visit the Botanical Gardens, the Coliseum, and then I'm making the long pilgrimage to Minho.'

This little tale has been repeated countless times. The woman feels a need to tell it, to unburden and so to comfort herself:

Andresa can sense the grief borne by her compatriot.

'He couldn't withstand the journey. Two days after we arrived, he died at the Colonial Hospital in Ultramar.'

'Poor thing', says Andresa, just for something to say. As if the conversation should not simply end there.

'It's true. Such terrible luck.'

She takes the handkerchief out of her bag and holds it to her nose again.

'It's true.' The woman still has more to unburden. 'A whole lifetime spent thinking about coming to Lisbon, a whole lifetime imagining that trip, and in the end...'

Lowering her eyes, Andresa adjusts her skirt. It has inched up, exposing her bony knees.

'You don't remember my father, do you?'

'No', confesses Andresa. 'To be honest with you I don't really remember him. You know, it's over fifteen years since I left the island.'

'Too true, too true.'

Then in a different tone of voice:

'My father was Simão Filili from Alto de Celarine.'

'Ah! Nhô Simão Filili was your father then? I thought you were his niece.' (She is lying.)

'It was me and my sister Zinha, God rest her soul. I'm Tanha. We were his only daughters.'

'I remember Zinha perfectly. I had it for a fact you were cousins' (another little lie to complete the bouquet). 'She was very pretty.'

'She was, poor soul.'

Now, at last, Andresa has more or less gathered up the threads, and feels more at ease. Who could forget that wrinkled little old man from the red house over on Alto de Celarine? Only someone who had never heard the tales of the *gongon*.* Tales of blustery nights and chains dragged along the road to Pontinha under the dark powers of the *xuxo*.† Horses that thundered across the property in the early hours. Villagers would always mention the ear-splitting sound of horses' hooves clattering on stony paths. They were on their way to worship at the tomb of nhô Rei Vendido,

---

* *gongon*: monkey or jungle god
† *xuxo*: evil spell or treachery

the Betrayed King. In a voice choked with fear, Nha Xenxa, widow of nhô João Sena, told of how on one occasion she had heard a voice coming from the midst of the thunderous galloping. And she'd recognized it all too well. It was the voice of nhô Simão Filili commanding: 'Rein in my father's stallion! Bring my spurs, my fine spurs, my girth, my saddle!' It was the dead of night and nha Xenxa was trapped in a nightmare, ladies and gentlemen! She only calmed down when her daughter, woken by nha Xenxa's moaning, applied a few powerful slaps.

Andresa studies her compatriot, seated there beside her. She has such a defeated look to her. As though life were merely passing her by without her even noticing. She peers curiously at Tanha's smooth complexion, seemingly haunted by dark shadows, even darker than her coffee-coloured skin, lending her eyes a nostalgic melancholy. How old would Tanha be? In her thirties? Nonsense, she must be well into her forties. Without doubt. From her schooldays she remembers Tanha as a ripe young woman who flirted from the window of her town house with a young man from Santo Antão, son of nhô Pedro and nha Mari Barba, and an incorrigible drunk. The hangovers he used to wake up with! You really had to hand it to him. Hangovers bound to have unsettled anybody. Then he would start mud-slinging: *this one's mother is a so-and-so, the father of that one is a such-and-such, she's a spinster's daughter! you're nothing but a bastard, that fellow never even married your mother!* Whoever happened to be passing at that moment would receive a dose of his medicine. *You're just another stuck-up nobody. Sit down over there, sit down.* Folk might laugh but they fled the young man from Santo Antão. An undeniably insolent youth! As you know, there's plenty of grog on Santo Antão, so youths got used to drinking, and the result was this spectacle of mud-slinging at any innocent Christian who crosses their path.

Moved by a curiosity she can't properly explain, Andresa asks:

'Are you here alone?'

Tanha raises her eyes and turns to face Andresa with a friendly smile, the smile of people from the islands when they encounter acquaintances, compatriots, and old friends.

'Well at least now my brother Julio is here. Julio became a doctor, and he's married. He got married to a girl from here. To a *mondronga*.'*

Andresa is taken aback:

'Your brother has already qualified? I had no idea.'

'Oh, yes', and Tanha smiles in satisfaction. 'He finished his course four years ago. I could have stayed at my brother's house, but I prefer living with my cousins in Oeiras.'

* * *

* *mondronga*: hideous woman or witch

Lowering her voice, she confides:

'*Mondrongas* are too bossy. I'm much more comfortable with my cousins.'

Andresa smiles. She keeps smiling and looking down the empty platform. It is that dead period of the afternoon when the trains carries only half a dozen passengers. They spread themselves out through the carriages, patiently waiting for the moment to depart.

A train draws into the platform and comes to a stop just in front of them. Tanha stands up and runs a hand over her skirt to smooth it. She clutches her bag and her gloves, looking awkward.

'This must be the one.'

'Must be', agrees Andresa. 'But it shouldn't leave for another ten minutes.'

'Yes, but I think I'll get going. I'll feel more comfortable.'

She is smiling again. Her black hair, pulled tight and secured with clips, gives her the air of a sphinx.

Andresa accompanies her for a few final moments.

'You know, I could go with you. I live in Caxias. But I need to wait for my husband.'

She falls silent. Deep down inside she is annoyed with herself. There I go with my explanations. I seem to spend my whole life doing it. I'm not going with her because I'm not the slightest bit interested. Enough of the chitchat.

She calmly enters the bar and asks for a coffee. She will have to wait half an hour for the next train. She sips the hot liquid. It tastes good.

Back on the platform, she lights a cigarette and sits down on the same bench as before.

Although springtime has arrived, late afternoons are still grey and sultry. Yet the empty platform seems somehow brighter now.

Andresa is unable to figure out what prevented her from accompanying Tanha. She is genuinely waiting for her husband, but it isn't a problem. She could have gone further on down the line with Tanha, reminiscing about old times, listening to her recount the latest news in the sweet and easy lilt of São Vicente.

The cigarette, forgotten between her fingers, has grown a long grey tail of ash.

It's been a while now since this started happening to her. She sees one of her compatriots and feels the need to talk to them, to build a bridge which will remind her of her people, her land. But as soon as the contact is made, disappointment begins to take over. Something deep inside makes her feel this way. She doesn't feel any affinity with people from fifteen years ago. They aren't the same as they were. She bumps into them here and there, in Rossio, in Estrela, scattered about Lisbon, in Camões Square on Sunday mornings, in Conde Barão, in Cais do Sodré Station.

If nhô Simão Filili were still alive, he would no doubt have remained the same imposing and mythical figure as always. He was one of a kind! Everybody knew nhô Simão Filili. Old Pegleg Filili, whispered the youngsters.

A red-headed English woman with a cane sits down next to her.

Andresa flicks away her cigarette and crosses her legs.

She first met nhô Simão Filili on a sweltering hot day.

On that scorching afternoon, she had set out to return a copy of Eça de Queiroz' periodical *The Barbs*, which her father had borrowed. She came across him sitting on a bench by the door to his house, using the end of his cane to poke holes and trace lines in the earth.

Shrunken, probably due to a surfeit of hunger and deprivation, he had in addition an idiosyncratic manner of speaking. It startled anybody who hadn't heard it before. The words rolled around his mouth like shingle dragged along the shore by churning waves. In the end, they emerged, loose and disconnected, but always deliberate. It was said that he spoke like this because he was a Mason. Locals confirmed it was most certainly down to Freemasonry. He meddled in the dark arts, just like the sorceresses did. All he was missing was a tail, one of those the witches of Tchad Além kept hidden under their long skirts, or the monkeys up at Travessa do Monte. When it came to nha Chica Maçaroca, the witch of Achada, you could almost *see* the end of her tail dragging through the dusty streets. And the children would be rocked to sleep with their nannies singing: *nha Chica Maçaroca ta buli ta bai, ta buli ta bem.*

It was the elderly housemaid Bia Antónia who supplied Andresa with these and other tall tales. After dinner, Bia Antónia would sit on a box at the bottom of the stairs to the verandah overlooking the yard. In between drawing on a pipe that always hung from a corner of her mouth, the servant would delve into her horde of stories. Andresa, leaning on the verandah, listened to her absentmindedly.

Bia Antónia spoke with conviction.

'If a man wants to become a Mason, his first test is to walk barefoot over a bed of needles. They say, Miss, that nhô Simão Filili performed this task like no one else. As he approached closer to the bed of needles, there came a thundering of hooves. Sounded like fine-people horses, *cataboom, cataboom*. Teeth clenched, he didn't look back, and the horses still went *cataboom, cataboom*. But nhô Simão Filili, wild-eyed, clothes torn, saliva running, hands stinging, he never once looked back.'

Bia Antónia sucked greedily on the slow-burning pipe resting forgotten in the corner of her mouth.

'And then?' asked Andresa.

The old servant raised her myopically bulging eyes towards Andresa and replied:

'Now, they say he conjures up a fog of war every night over Pontinha.'

'What kind of talk is this, Bia Antónia?'

'Yes ma'am, it's the truth. Using Masonic arts he's summoning up a fog of war on the stroke of midnight. People seen him, all garbed in white. Nha Xenxa lives just above Pontinha and she feels it all through the blessed night. It's a dragging of chains and it's nhô Simão Filili screaming all night long at his drowning sailors.'

'But has nha Xenxa ever seen him?' asked an incredulous Andresa.

'No ma'am, nha Xenxa is a good Christian. She counts her blessings and says her prayers, but oh, those Masons, they have gone and made a pact with the *xuxo*.'

Andresa enjoyed listening to the stories spread by the villagers' word of mouth. And the villagers put so much faith in them that nhô Simão Filili soon became feared and respected from one end of the island to the other.

The biggest commotion was on the day Zinha died. No one would ever forget it. What happened became the talk of afternoons and long evenings in the houses around the neighbourhood for a long time, and that's when everybody became truly convinced he really was a Mason. And the circle of legends around nhô Simão Filili grew ever wider.

Zinha had been sick with a mysterious disease for several months. Her skin had turned dull and taken on a greyish hue. Her fiancé often travelled to Guinea, and this set the villagers whispering. A sickness like this could only have come from a hex cast by his black lover in Bissau. Didn't you know? A Guinean will curse someone for next to nothing. It was hardly a new situation: any single man abroad would get himself a girl, and often one or two children, before eventually marrying someone else. As for Zinha, hex or no hex, the truth is that she was ill. But hex or no hex, the truth is that many young people on São Vicente died of tuberculosis or, if they were still children, of typhoid fever or, if they were still young infants, then they died of dysentery. So why was everybody spreading all this foolish gossip?

They discussed it in hushed tones, until one day the news went round the streets like wildfire, nobody knows exactly how. Zinha had sent a telegram to her fiancé breaking off their engagement. Nobody mentioned it, but the town approved. Yes, ma'am. It was the only way to get rid of the curse affecting the sick girl. Yet it did nothing to prevent Zinha from succumbing soon after, early one morning before the cock crowed twice.

Tanha then started to go down with fits, when she foamed at the mouth, and yelled loud enough for the whole neighbourhood to learn that her father hadn't consented to a visit from the priest to perform her sister's last rites. But there was already a rumour running in the village. There was to be a religious funeral after all.

Andresa recalls all these events yet it seems as though they never actually happened, still less that she bore witness to them. Another time, late at night, Bia Antónia sat in her usual place, on the box at the foot of the stairs leading into the yard, unravelling the rest of this *gongon* story.

'Listen, Miss', and the housekeeper took two pulls on the stem of her half-extinguished pipe. 'Listen. When nhô Padre arrived at the door of nhô Simão Filili's house, he found himself unable to enter.'

Andresa continued staring at the long date-palm fronds, drooping and sweeping in the mild nocturnal breeze, up against the pulley secured with hemp ropes to the three-piece scaffold over the mouth of the well.

'This house is haunted, miss.'

Bia Antónia scratched her head under her shawl, and then carried on in the same tone of voice:

'Nhô Simão Filili called for the entrance and walls of the room where the coffin was laid to be lined with palm fronds. Then he waited for nhô Padre. Ah—and as well he clutched a large branch against his chest, his arms crossed tightly over it.'

The wind blew more forcefully and Bia Antónia huddled deeper into her striped smock. Andresa allowed a watery gob of spit to drop down onto the stones in the yard.

'When the nhô Padre arrived and saw all those Masonic trappings, he turned his back, without even crossing the threshold. House excommunicated! They say Miss Tanha was worn out with crying. The funeral took place round back of the church, you know. Oh, and in the procession were two guitars and a violin and they played bittersweet *mornas* all the way to the cemetery.'*

She placed her hands on her knees and hauled herself up off the box where she had been sitting with difficulty. Bringing her hands up to her flanks, she rested them there and, as if performing a gentle stretch, raised herself up onto the tips of her bare toes. Moments later, she added:

'Everybody in the procession cried and cried. No doubt but that she was well wept over.'

Andresa recalls all of this in as much detail as if it had happened only yesterday. As if she had never been separated from her motherland and was still walking in the footsteps of nhô Simão Filili, nhô Faia, Antoninho Ligório, and Pitra.

Beside her, the red-headed English woman continues to share her bench.

Here in the empty station, she finally notices the train.

She stands up and begins to walk. When she reaches the second carriage, she peers in. Tanha, appearing relaxed and her face serene, huddles in a corner of her seat as if to make room for at least five other passengers. She smiles up at Andresa.

Poor old Tanha. I'll go with her as far as Caxias.

---

* *morna*: traditional slow tempo music from Cape Verde, usually played on guitar, cavaquinho and other instruments

Still Life with Head of Bream

Teolinda Gersão

So, as planned, I went to pick up Rui today at ten thirty. Instead of phoning from the car as usual and waiting for the housekeeper to bring him down, I rang the bell and went up.

Otilia would be bound to invite me in—you always ask a visitor to enter and Otilia, although a housekeeper, would have been well aware of the basic rules of etiquette.

It was Rui who came to the front door, took me by the hand, and pulled me inside.

'Come and see my train, Dad.' The train was laid out on his bedroom floor and began to run smoothly along the tracks as soon as he flicked the switch.

I sat down on the carpet next to Rui, and offered what I thought were relevant comments. A model train can be a cherished toy, capable of bringing fathers and sons together for hours in the same enraptured contemplation. At least that's the way it is in the adverts. I looked round and there it was, the radiant image on the cardboard box where the pieces were kept: a smiling blond child, and a cheery young man. A Dad.

I tried hard to mimic the advertisement, because surely that's what Rui expected of me. But I have to admit that I was never very excited by model trains—maybe that's why I'd never thought of giving him one. Electric trains and Meccano sets seemed like relics of the past, a time when there were no computers, computerized toys, or other miracles of technology.

I did my best to demonstrate some enthusiasm and affected to admire the locomotive and the carriages which Rui would re-attach every time the train stopped.

For his part, on the other hand, the enthusiasm was unmistakably genuine.

'Do you see, Dad? It's going so fast! And now there's going to be a crash!'

But there wasn't, because at the very last moment he burst out laughing, then stretched out his hand and snatched up the carriage that had halted and blocked the track.

'Brilliant, brilliant', I kept saying, while crossing and uncrossing my legs, because sitting cross-legged on the floor was far from comfortable for legs as long as mine.

'Now go and put your coat on', I told him once I felt this had gone on long enough. 'We're going out'.

The train made three or four more circuits with Rui on all fours, racing alongside the track or sitting beside it, waiting for the train to come around by itself.

'Great, now put the pieces away', I finally said, determined not to hang about any longer, and I helped to put it all back in the box.

'How's it going at school?'

'Fine, Dad', he answered, without interest.

I didn't insist.

'I'll wait for you in the living room', I told him. 'Go and put on your coat.'

I sat down on the sofa. So this was it, then, the very living room into which I'd decided I would venture today— and which I now no longer recognized. Different furniture, ornaments, and wall-hangings, different sofas and curtains. All of which was, in fact, only to be expected, since this was no longer my home. The apartment now belonged to Rui's mother and her current husband. I was entering it for the first time since the divorce, safe in the knowledge that they had left Lisbon for the weekend.

Naturally, they were free to change the living room, I thought, as I glanced around. Just as they had been free to change their life.

I had nothing do with that—although I was at least partly implicated. Or had been. Because they had changed my life as well. And I wasn't altogether convinced that they had the right.

Fine, that was her decision. Manuela's. She hadn't lied, she hadn't made a scene.

'It's hopeless', she had said. 'You and me—it doesn't work. In any case, I've met someone else.' That was that.

'I've met somebody else, so open the door and leave, from now on this apartment is mine alone, I'm keeping the apartment. Keeping the apartment and keeping Rui. The apartment and Rui are mine.' No, that's not what she had said.

'Not Rui, no. Rui will always belong to both of us,' I protested. But that was just what she had said too. 'Rui will always belong to both of us.'

In fact, if I'm being honest I have to acknowledge that she was being perfectly civilized. The money and the assets, including the apartment, were all subject to negotiation. Rigorously split in half.

But Rui. Rui couldn't be split in half, yet the time we each spent with him could be. Joint custody was the term employed. A fortnight in one apartment, a fortnight in the other.

I was the one who eventually relented regarding the terms, coming to collect him just at weekends, or even, like today, just on a Sunday, because I often had to work Saturdays. In practice the arrangement seemed to work for all of us. I have a very responsible position, as Manuela is well aware, and by the end of the day I'm usually exhausted, and children wear you out. Or maybe I just haven't got the knack, although my love for Rui has never been in doubt. And as Manuela has also always been well aware.

'It would be a power struggle if I asked to keep Rui the whole time', I had said to Manuela, here in this very living room. 'You were always the one who looked after him. If I laid claim to him now it would be a fight against you rather than for him. But I don't want to get into a fight with you. Let's keep it civilized.'

'I agree', she said. 'For five years you've had the same opportunities as I to take him to school and collect him back again, dress and undress him, feed him, give him a bath, play with him, put him to bed, bring him to his appointments with the paediatrician and the dentist. You hardly ever did any of those things, always preferring to watch television or read the paper. It would be absurd to get into a fight now to regain the right to something that you didn't want before. Let's have an amicable divorce.'

'Dad, I'm ready', says Rui, coming in with his coat on. 'Where are we going today?'

'To the Oceanarium', I suggest. 'How about it?'

'I'm going to the Oceanarium', Rui yells to Otilia, running halfway down the corridor before coming back to pull me by the hand.

He's the one who presses the lift button on the way down.

'You've got a new car', he exclaims, seeming surprised and happy. 'I like your new car, Dad.'

'That's terrific', Otilia had said when Rui told her about the Oceanarium.

And at the door she informed me:

'I'll be back at the apartment by seven, Sir. You can bring the boy home whenever you like. So long as it's after seven.'

The clock on the dashboard says eleven-thirty. So we have seven-and-a-half hours, Rui and I.

It's a mild day, neither hot nor cold. And it's February. No wind, and sun between the clouds. I drive quickly. It's a powerful car and has an automatic gear shift. There's very little traffic on the road, the only irritation being the fact that they never programme the traffic lights conveniently. It's absurd to have to spend the same time waiting for them to change on Sundays as you do during the week.

'Have you been on the cable-car?' I ask, and Rui's face lights up.

'Yeah. With Mum and David. Are we going there again, Dad? Can we do it again?'

'Alright', I say, 'We can do it again.'

We're on the airport roundabout and turn off towards the Parque das Nações.

Mum and David, I think. Okay, Mum can live with David. But he can't take my place. I'm going to be Rui's Dad for the rest of my life. I like spending time with him and he likes spending time with me.

We both enjoy riding in the cable-car. Up there, I feel a long way from the everyday. Seen from above like this, things appear different. It occurs to me that everything in life could just be a matter of perspective.

It's almost one o'clock, so we have lunch in a Pizza Hut. Rui's choice, naturally. I hate pizza, but I go along with it. Although it's still early, the restaurant is full. There are a lot of tourists as well as those out for a typical Sunday stroll. Mostly families.

We order a Four Seasons pizza and a smaller one with mozzarella, along with a peach juice and a beer. Whitney Huston is singing in the background. Or maybe Mariah Carey, I don't know. Manuela was always the one who knew all the songs.

Is it true that we know we are old when we no longer know who's singing the songs—on the radio, in the background music in cafés?

They take a long time to serve us and Rui begins to grow restless. At a nearby table a family take their seats: Dad,

Mum, and a little blond girl with an enormous doll that, at a quick glance, looks alive. At the table next to ours two young men are drinking beer. Then they get up and go, leaving a triangle of pineapple and anchovy pizza on the board. I reach out an arm, pick up the slice and start eating it, shamelessly, while Rui bursts into laughter, delighted to see Dad doing something you're not supposed to. I laugh too, and offer him a piece, which he enthusiastically takes in his hand.

When they finally serve us and I start drinking the beer, I have the sensation that life may actually be falling into place. That if we don't get too wound up, things find their own strange way of working themselves out.

We finally head off to the Oceanarium, wandering down dark corridors which make us feel as though we're at the bottom of the sea. Yet always on the other side of a pane of glass.

Rui wants to see everything—brightly coloured fish, sharks, penguins, sea otters. I think he's most taken by the penguins' high-speed dives and by the fuzzy sea otters, who embrace one another as they swim, and look like stuffed toys.

By the time we leave it's almost six o'clock. We still have time for an ice cream in the Vasco de Gama shopping centre, and then take turns on a computer we find on a different floor, each of us printing our own visitor's card with our names (Rui, Edgar) in different fonts, selected from a menu. After that I write on my card: Edgar, Dad of Rui. And on his card: Rui, son of Edgar.

Meantime, it's turned seven o'clock and I take Rui home.

'Come on in, Dad', he says. 'Come upstairs and play with me.'

I tell him I have to finish some work and leave him with Otilia.

'I'll pick you up on Saturday, and we'll spend Saturday and Sunday together. I promise. And on Sunday I'll cook something for the two of us in my apartment. Something great, you'll see.'

I hug him tightly then return to the car. This time my work is a lie. I could have gone in—but I don't want to go back into that apartment again. I won't be going back inside that apartment anytime soon.

Suddenly I feel empty. I try to distract myself and begin thinking about what I'll cook on Sunday, lunch for just the two of us. I'll have to ask Laura. I don't know why I made Rui any such promise. I've never cooked and I don't know how I'll manage. But there has to be a first time. And it shouldn't be that difficult, for example steaks and spaghetti. Or oven chips. I'll ask Laura. She'll probably think that I'm having a woman over. But isn't it usually women who hone their cooking skills for men? I didn't imagine I'd ever cook for a woman. But I am going to cook for the two of us, Rui and me.

I parked the car, but didn't feel like going straight up to my apartment. I walked another couple of blocks, bought some cigarettes, had a coffee, started walking again, and wandered into a gallery showing three or four sculptures and some paintings. I glanced at them without interest. However, one of them caught my attention, maybe for being a sort of modern pastiche of a Flemish painting, or something like that. I'm no art connoisseur. It depicted a table with a basket of fruit, and next to it a dish of whelks, seaweed, and stones with an enormous, glassy-eyed fish in the foreground. The caption, posted next to it on the wall in tiny letters, was *Still Life with Head of Bream.*

I didn't think too much about it afterwards. I went home, had a piece of toast, tidied up some paperwork, made a few phone calls, listened to the news bulletin, watched part of a film, took a hot shower, prepared a glass of juice, and took a sleeping pill. But I knew the painting would return to my memory, and I knew it would remain there, for no apparent reason, until I fell asleep.

Collectors

Mário de Carvalho

The antique-collecting bug is something that comes and goes. This is the tale of what one day befell my friend Diniz Álvares, weary of monotonous late-night sessions at the film society, tired of a youth wasted on collecting filmographies and lecturing small somnolent audiences on the significance of Dreyer.

Despite what they tell you, not everyone is capable of everything. I know fellows who, with a knowledgeable air, insist on talking through a restaurant's wine list and yet, when pressed, can't distinguish between two vintages of *Evel Branco*. I know of others, from musical families, who were tortured during childhood with Saint Saëns' études, who can converse at length about that time Richter came to São Carlos, and yet can't stay awake through the second movement of Kodály's *Peacock Variations*. And yet others who, whilst calling themselves dog breeders, can't differentiate a cocker from a springer spaniel, no matter how many times you explain it to them. And there are still more, self-proclaimed art lovers devourers of monographs, exhibitions, and museums, who are unable to tell a Pedro Alexandrino from a Domingos Sequeira, unless it happens to correspond to one of their recently consulted reproductions.

Unfortunately, my friend Diniz Álvares belonged to that group of people with plenty of talent for running film societies, but very little for the collecting of bric-a-brac, and unworthy of the exorbitantly priced books and catalogues he scrutinized so patiently—even arduously—during peaceful weekends spent in his dressing gown and slippers.

In the grip of this new obsession, Diniz would frequently come to consult me and soak up my words—which I strained to make sound erudite—with an anxious, enraptured air.

Amongst my friends I had acquired the unfortunate reputation of being knowledgeable. For many years I had lived in a very foolish but highly refined environment. Rare was the day during my childhood when my aristocratic father would arrive home without a unique piece of Lalique glassware, a painted panel from Sardoal, a fragment of baroque carving, or an Afghan hound. Until finally, when it was already far too late, the law intervened and put an end to his prodigality. But by that point our house in Graça had become a hive of officials who repossessed everything. And when my father eventually died, it was in a tiny flat in the run-down Reboleira district, prostrate on a four-poster bed with his arms wrapped around a fifteenth-century marble cross which had somehow escaped the bailiffs.

In his blind obstinacy, my father had been unable to imagine any role in life for me other than that of a priest or a soldier. As I demonstrated little vocation for either profession, he decided, grudgingly, that I should simply live off the family fortune. Yet he took it upon himself, with his daily squandering, to frustrate even that one remaining prospect.

So I had to get a job, with no skills that would allow me to advance beyond the role of a third-rate bookkeeper. I soon found myself a nameless employee at a municipal library in Penha da França and, on top of that, a translator of soporific tomes for the Academy of Sciences. I was, therefore, at least putting to modest use the seven ghastly years I'd spent at the Lycée Français.

My new acquaintances quickly gathered that I had only a minor talent for film societies and literary reviews, but soon granted me great authority on the subject of knowing-things-people-don't-usually-know.

My daily handling of books allowed me to organize and systematize the memories from my childhood, and so to consolidate the affectionate prestige bestowed upon me by my friend Diniz, the budding collector, throughout those avid and insistent consultations.

One day, Diniz came round to my house unexpectedly, without calling beforehand as he usually did. He was carrying a long roll of paper which he unfurled exuberantly on top of my large Louis XIII writing desk. I could sense that he'd been dying of impatience to show me his latest acquisition.

It was a map.

He told me he'd seen it for the first time in the window of an antiquarian bookshop on Rua do Alecrim, just below Praça das Flores, and that he'd decided to buy it then and there. The antiquarian bookshop, however, was always closed, so that he went to Rua do Alecrim often, and returned home just as often dispirited, without so much as seeing the map up close. Finally, on one occasion, when having abandoned all hope, he was once again walking down Rua do Alecrim, he noticed the door was ajar.

He was served by a surly, and very grubby, hunchbacked German, who reluctantly agreed to show him the map, and handed it over equally reluctantly when, without even querying the price, Diniz pulled out a cheque for the exorbitant sum mentioned. At the door, having meticulously wrapped up the purchase, the German, in his hair-raising accent, advised taking extra-special care of the map. In his euphoria, my friend took this remark as an intrusive but well-meaning display of the dedication of an old connoisseur whose soul had been pierced by the loss of a precious object.

I took some time in the process of disappointing Diniz. On the one hand, I wanted to avoid causing him a sudden shock, and on the other, to uphold the generally held belief in my critical sensibility for such matters.

I was painstaking in my examination of the map, which consisted of a meandering inspection with a magnifying glass and persistent checking of folios of serious appearance. Finally, regretfully, I delivered my verdict. The map was an unquestionable forgery.

Defiantly, Diniz pressed a trembling finger against the faded inscription of an unintelligible Flemish name, and the location of Scheveningen, 1709.

I explained—with a perverse pleasure, I confess—that there was no cartographer with that name listed in any of the specialist books, that there had never been a map produced in Scheveningen, and that, furthermore, it had never been a practice of cartographers to indicate the location of a map's origin.

There followed a decisive argument that dashed any remaining hope of the map being greeted as an archaeological find. It was that all the contours of the landmasses were rigorously correct, inconsistent with the irregularities, imprecisions, and gaps in cartography from the first half of the eighteenth century.

Then I spent a good deal of time demonstrating my thesis. In the hands of my subdued friend I placed reproductions of old maps, from Al-Idrisi, Toscanelli, and Juan de la Cosa, to those of Pedro and Jorge Reinel, Luís Teixeira, Cipriano Vilacêncio, Diogo Homem, and Vaz Dourado, as well as the Dutch portulan charts of Hondius, Blavius, and Janszoon Waghenaer, pointing out the distortions in comparison to a modern *Larousse Atlas*. I drew my friend's attention to the fact that the date marked on his map, which was previous to the meditations of La Condamine and Maupertuis, the stabilization of the pendulum by George Graham, and the precision which was only then introduced into calculation, could be nothing less than fantastical. And that, as such, his acquisition, which would hold up so well against a world map in any modern classroom, must itself be a fantasy. Or better yet: an utter fake.

And, definitive and accusatory, my index finger circled Australia, which the inattentive counterfeiter had reproduced in its entirety, on a map supposedly prior to the voyages of Bougainville and Cook.

Furthermore, the map was lavishly illuminated, in shades of green and brown, with ships, sea monsters, unicorns, and flags, whose design had clearly been stencilled from fifteenth-century motifs, again anachronous to the attested date.

In short, I drew my case for its being a forgery to a brilliant conclusion, while letting it be known that further arguments could be incorporated into my already lengthy exposition. And based on the ink utilized, the delineation of the illuminations, and on subtle and inconsistent Art Nouveau flourishes, I dated the map, with some reservations, to some period in the twenties or early thirties of this century.

Diniz sank feebly onto the sofa, crestfallen, overwhelmed by the evidence of this deception. He made a vague gesture of resignation, waving a limp and lifeless hand, and sat there, breathing heavily, eyes fixed upon his knees.

I realized then that it was time to console him, raise his spirits, after having dragged him into the depths of disenchantment. I was pleasant, gracious, and I brought through a tray of drinks.

Sitting opposite him, I proposed that, although a forgery many times over, the map was still not entirely divested of value, even if it was true that it certainly wasn't worth the sum my friend had parted with so lightly. It shouldn't be left to languish, carelessly rolled up in the corner of a room. On the contrary, as long as it were properly referenced and demystified, it would have its place in a collection.

And I told him of the case of a relative of mine who once upon a time, in Spain, bought a wrought silver hourglass that the seller guaranteed was a rare piece by Benvenuto Cellini. But it was a fake: neither silver, nor by Cellini. So what did my relative do? Did he let his spirits drop? Did he hide the piece away in the corner of an attic, between broken armchairs and rusty candelabras? Well, of course not. Instead, he began collecting Cellini forgeries wherever he could find them, and, by the end of his life, had accumulated thousands of pieces, falsified in the most varied locations and for the most disparate purposes. His collection of *Perseus* miniatures alone numbered forty-two...

Then I stood up, rummaged behind a set of encyclopaedias and brought out a dusty violin which I placed in Diniz's hands. I had him read the consecrated inscription, stuck inside the resonance chamber:

Antonius Stradivarius Cremonensis faciebat anno 1725.

But this wasn't an authentic Stradivarius we were looking at. It had been bought by a monastery's novice master from a gypsy in Vila Viçosa, at the beginning of the century. And, in spite of this, it was an object worth owning.

Then I recalled the enormous collection of fake Stradivarii kept by the Count of Schnitzell-Barros at his property in Azeitão. Each one of them, in the darkness of its interior, displaying the same inscription, albeit with differences in date—some from after the death of the illustrious Cremonese—typeface, printing process, size, and contour. The fact remains that some of those counterfeit violins produce an excellent sound.

And that night, already deep into the early hours, my friend left me feeling consoled by the prospect of a newly inaugurated collection of falsified maps.

It was a long time before Diniz Álvares came to see me again. And he didn't return under the best circumstances. He burst into the house, visibly disturbed, breathless, and waving a crumpled newspaper. I calmed him down as best I could, sat him down, fixed him a soothing cocktail of vermouth, brandy, and strong tea, then prepared to listen to his story.

A few days earlier, on the birthday of his youngest son, there had been a party at his house, a rowdy gathering of friends and their children. I had, in fact, been invited, but had managed to wriggle out of it with some excuse or other. Playing the good host, Diniz had shown off his antiques and had practically glowed, exhibiting the map on top of a table and commenting knowledgeably on its imperfections, based on my own previous account.

After his audience had dispersed, he noticed on rolling up the map that someone had left a red wine stain on its surface, and that the hand of a mischievous child had traced around this in a felt-tip pen. Although annoyed, he resolved to clean the map in the coming days, and didn't attach too much importance to the incident.

However, over the following week, he was shocked by the news on the radio of the sudden appearance of a huge island, as large as Tasmania, between the Tubuai and Kermadec archipelagos, at approximately longitude 158°E and latitude 28°S. The Australian government had immediately staked its claim to the island and proceeded with the occupation of that enormous territory, apparently constituting a vast expanse of solidified lava. It was the first time that, from one day to the next, an island had emerged from the sea without any previous signs of volcanic activity. And this caused a buzz in the scientific community, of which the newspapers gave a modest account, and which my friend accompanied with a sense of growing discomfort.

The thing was, he confessed in anguish, the location of the new island (he had spent hours confirming the exact coordinates with a compass and set square) could be perfectly and irrefutably matched to the wine stain on his map.

I could only laugh at my friend's distress. I asked him whether he didn't think it a bit much to imagine himself in possession of divine powers of creation, and sought to appease him by narrating various stories, some real, others invented, of extraordinary coincidences.

But this didn't appear to reassure him. He paced back and forth across my living room, lost in thought, issuing puffs of cigar smoke, and muttering, between gritted teeth: 'Oh Christ, oh Christ.'

To settle the matter once and for all, and so he'd be able to sleep easy, I offered to go to his home that same night and conduct a conclusive experiment.

He drove me in his car, glum, heedless of pedestrian crossings, indifferent to traffic lights. A short while later he was unfolding the map on a table, regarding me with a wary look and pointing to the purplish stain which supposedly indicated the new island.

Ignoring his panicked gestures, I picked up a pen and drew a sort of lopsided, irregular ellipsis right in the middle of the Atlantic Ocean, between the Azores and the Bermuda Islands, which I proceeded to fill in completely with a green felt-tip. And then, leaving my friend in suspense, I returned home, where I slept soundly.

The next day, however, the news had spread across the entire city. An enormous island—or, more precisely, a new continent—had appeared suddenly, to the west of the Azores, supplanting the Sargasso Sea and leaving the ocean liners in the area lying high and dry.

The newspaper headlines were dramatic and unsettling: 'NEW CONTINENT SOUTHWEST OF AZORES', 'RETURN OF ATLANTIS?', 'PLANET GROWS RESTLESS'. And in the subheadings: 'There has been no change in tides, confirms Lisbon Meteorological Institute', 'Will Portugal claim new territory?', 'Interview with captain of *Balduíno II* oil tanker who witnessed strange phenomenon', '*Terra de Fogo* and *Harlém* ships still missing', 'Portuguese Airforce conducts reconnaissance of new continent', 'Matias de Menezes of National Laboratory for Civil Engineering expresses doubts—These islands are ephemeral'.

Judging by the accounts, the new continent was arid, black, and seemed to be volcanic. By the end of the day, volcanologist Haroun Tazieff had announced from Paris that he would be departing for the new territory in a helicopter that very night. Meanwhile, the Portuguese Navy's *Fernão Mendes Pinto* was raising the national flag to the east of the island, despite the Minister of Foreign Affairs declaring from Lisbon that it was far too early to advance territorial claims.

This time, it was I who showed up on Diniz's doorstep. He hadn't even made it in to work. In contrast to my misplaced confidence of the previous evening, he had been wandering about his house all night, unable to get a wink of sleep, in the anticipation of what had eventually come to pass.

He greeted me coldly. Then, with the map spread across the table, he sadistically made me watch as he compared the coordinates of my indiscretion from the night before against those that were being broadcast on every news bulletin. They were exactly and incontrovertibly the same.

He reprimanded me for my excessive self-confidence and, on more than one occasion, crossed the line of decency. He asked me, sarcastically, what I intended to do from here on in, and whether I would entertain myself with the collection of magical islands and continents.

Somewhat calmer, and conscious of our shared burden of complicity, he proposed not mentioning this subject to anybody, concealing our part in the global disturbance, and returning the map to the German antiquarian book dealer.

I opposed this. And I also opposed the idea of burning the map in the living room fireplace, alerting Diniz to the potentially dramatic consequences, given the circumstances.

After some discussion as to the best destination for the map, I made my friend an offer which he accepted with great relief: I would take the map home myself and bury it among my papers. And with this we parted, each of us convinced that it would be some time before we saw each other again.

These days I contemplate the map on the broad surface of my desk. I gently run my fingers along the contours of its continents and touch the new, recently created territories. With the tip of my nail I scratch lightly over Africa.

My eyes are fixed on the scalpel lying nearby. I imagine
what might happen if I were to scrape Africa, or America,
or Australia from the surface of the map. And the small
blade fascinates me. The attraction of the madman for the
axe, the yearning of the suicide for the abyss...

Metro Zoo

Hélia Correia

'You should bring your price down', they would say. And she found this amusing. 'Believe me, this is as low as I can go.' Haggling was part of the game. Nothing would come of this conversation, and that was fine by them. The price would not drop, and the men would hitch up their trousers. The fact that they appeared with a wad of money in their back pocket told its own story, though at this stage of the proceedings their hands always became strangely awkward. The twenty Euro note refused to peel off the wad, sticking like glue to the rest, and they had to run a little saliva over their fingers, bring a certain intimacy into play. At this point the temperature rose, as if it had been waiting for the opportunity. Because they never mentioned requiring air conditioning, and you could forget about opening a window. The temperature took care of itself, rising and falling at will. The truth is the men enjoyed having to mop their brows with their worn handkerchiefs, old scraps of cloth that someone tucked into their pockets for them. Yet still they grumbled and, with a smile, asked for a discount. Patiently, she sent them on their way, but not before automatically checking the coast was clear. It was an unnecessary precaution. Just like in a novel, it was a detail that added to the sense of her exasperating nonchalance. Nobody in the building would ever dream of cold-shouldering her. 'All she does is treat the old fellows' corns and calluses', according to the old women in the local café. They were all aware of an air of beneficence they could never have anticipated only a few years earlier. In a way, they were all sisters trapped inside the same misfortune. Within the building, everybody became infused with an odour of animals.

* * *

She had given up advertising long ago. 'Blonde and easy-going', the ad had promised, so implying a certain expertise. But ads could be dangerous if they fell into the hands of greedy handlers. Men like that already checked her out, came into her home. 'This isn't a free market', they warned. She leaned forward to point out the greying roots of her hair. 'Not worth a thing', she assured them. And she raised her skirt so they could see the welts on her legs. They didn't seem convinced. 'Think girls like you can get by on nothing but the mercy of God?' She would play her penultimate card, flinging the window wide open for the smell to enter their nostrils, leaving them disgusted. 'Those who come once don't come back. Would you?'

One handler in particular, apparently happy with everything, wanted to be attended to right then and there. 'The truth is I've got this sickness', she said, showing him her medical report. The handler recognized the ruse but lacked the means to counter it. He drew himself up before hitting her with his ring, right where it would leave the most obvious mark. He was a short, efficient young man. She chose him without realizing it, and found herself talking percentages. 'Almost nobody comes here. And they pay next to nothing.'

He caressed the gold ring on his finger, like someone who knew how to deliberate. Flashed his well-kept teeth. You could always tell a pimp by his teeth. Every generation found a means to transfer their gains to the dentist. 'Move house and you'll earn more.'

'I'm not moving.'

He hit her again, with weary distaste. His high shirt collar, the colour of red paint, resembled a slit throat. 'Maybe', he considered aloud, 'it'll appeal to some people.'

She thought of contradicting him but kept quiet. In the street outside a speeding bus sent a jet of air wafting in through the window. For a brief moment the room was thick with a moribund odour.

'What did you say your name was?'

'Sandra.'

'Sandra. Yes. The ad says Idalette.'

'I bet no one would hit an Idalette', thought Sandra. And he could hear what she was thinking. Something was happening there, fomenting a crude mutual understanding, a bond between them. It dawned on her then that her former life spent avoiding the handlers had been one of fear. And she mistook simple relaxation and relief for the thrill of falling in love. But the young man didn't even tell her his name. 'I'll send someone round', he yelled on the way out. He was in a hurry. Perhaps it was the smell he was running away from. Sandra reckoned he would be back soon. But it was other people who came to collect the money, shifty criminals, little suited to the task. She asked to speak to the boss, but they answered that there was no boss. They worked for the syndicate. And Sandra recalled that blood-coloured throat, the ring which caught her right between the eyes. 'They must have killed him', she decided. That love story erased all the rest, beginning with the one about a wedding, and a honeymoon spent in poverty.

Her clientele remained more or less the same, attracted either by the old adverts, or tipped off by her regulars on where to enjoy such an indulgent ambience. Sandra would murmur 'Metro Zoo' down the phone, because none of them had the money for a taxi. 'You should bring your price down', they would say when it was over. Savouring the flavour of the phrase, reverting to the market place. In their weak-mindedness, they were saviours of a world fast approaching extinction. 'One of these days you'll be out of work. Young lads don't go for this sort of thing anymore.'

She wasn't easily offended. 'There are plenty of old men out there', she declared. 'Even when I'm dead, there will still be more than enough old fellows to go round.' She extended her arm and wiggled her fingers one after another, to wave them on their way, although she had nothing booked for the rest of the day. But, just as some felt the urge to wash themselves immediately afterwards, Sandra felt the need to give the animals her attention. Not that they wanted it, and they were almost certainly unaware of the effect they had on the demands of her schedule or the ebb and flow of her anxieties. However much she might desire it, they would never learn the truth about the smell that wafted into her little room of ill repute and the excitement it caused her. The only thing that the creatures and Sandra really shared was that faint hatred of humans, so faint, in fact, and with so little foundation, that it seemed almost more like a nervous tic, or a moral failing. For they were all very well taken care of, Sandra and the animals. None of them were at risk of cold or hunger.

She had stopped going there long ago. She remembered their eyes; screening the silent jungle, a jungle imprisoned behind a pane of glass. Sandra hadn't been raised to feel compassion. She had picked up chickens by their wings, carting them off to their death, thinking nothing of it. Others claimed that it was only with lambs that matters became complicated. That their meekness could break your heart; like someone who suddenly realizes that, in their sleep, they have murdered the person sharing their bed. But aside from this one uncomfortable example, there was nothing that could be described as a connection. Those with souls had souls, and the Lord simply told the rest: 'Thou shalt be eaten.' And they let themselves be eaten. To others He said: 'Thou shalt work.' And they worked. Never mind that cats, for example, do not hunt, or that dogs no longer guard our homes. At some point they were turned into children, demanding to be picked up and carried, getting fussy over their food. Sandra predicted that one day she too would toddle around clasping her cuddly toy, issuing tiny cries of delight. It was the fate of a woman without children, and even one with children once they no longer saw fit to come round and keep her company. For the time being, she resisted believing that a Christian might need to allow herself to get caught up in this kind of dilemma. Hers was a cheerful faith, sustained by religious medals inherited from a grandmother. Of the church, she knew no more than the chapel where the dead spent their last wake.

She would resolve all this in her old age, once fear descended and the smell of animals did, in fact, begin to disturb her.

Sandra had taken that apartment because its proximity to the zoo adversely affected its value, meaning it wasn't difficult to keep up with the rent. When the building was eventually sold off in sections, floor by floor, she began to worry about the Tenants' Committee meetings. To begin with, her neighbours had turned up their noses, their eyes looking past her, evading her like an obstacle. Social attitudes may have started to shift, moral ones not yet. But eventually consciences, too, grew resigned. It was Dona Idalette's life wasn't it? And she clearly paid her taxes for whatever exotic profession it was she engaged in. In addition, she was a kind woman, someone who understood common ailments and was able to rebuke the gluttons in the café. She also accompanied old ladies to the hospital, cancelling her morning appointments, something her work as a chiropodist fortunately allowed her to do. Even the priest preached tolerance to those old widows who carried their own mugs to the local café in their bags, assuming viruses from shared cups to be the miasma of sin. Taken literally, Idalette's 'easy life' merited the description. Good fortune had delivered the key right to her door.

All it would take would be to cross the old road humming with traffic, pay for an entrance ticket, and amble along those tree-lined pathways. But the truth is she no longer did this. A great divide seemed to separate the bodies of those animals from their enclosures, and what emerged was a soft moan, like water evaporating in the heat. Red-faced children, covered in dirt, beamed with incomprehension. 'Why? Why?' they kept asking. And their parents answered randomly. Against their will, they harboured unhappy memories of video footage showing people whose imprudence had led them right into the lions' den. 'Come along now,' the parents would say, before returning home, exhausted and ill-at-ease with themselves. They preferred it when the schools took them, all holding hands, on a study trip. The parents would suffer again later, around dawn, when dreams opened up precipices and a great truth took shape.

One morning she awoke feeling nauseous. She had run to the window, afraid of the symptom, in need of air. It had turned out to be a matter of no consequence, a minor failing in her generally healthy mechanism. But the thought of a pregnancy had begun a new flow of imagination. She would allow that child to grow inside her; she would give birth to it there, in the apartment; then, under cover of darkness, she would leave it in a little basket outside the gates. Outside those green gates behind which the nocturnal animals still kept their watch, on their solemn and senseless patrols. It was as if a suggestion had been a whispered in her ear, a whisper coming from her caged neighbours. There was plenty of warmth and milk to go around, they said. And that scent of dung and hide was impregnated with maternity.

Nothing had really happened inside Sandra, who was barren and knew it. The upset would leave no mark on her memory. Sleep had overtaken her forced wakefulness, offering some kind of treacherous consolation. But its false thread of empathy, almost a kind of trail—which for an instant intimated as real an existence as that of an invisible being over which a fine dust had settled, only disclosing its outline—never completely left her. She could no longer look on the animals as beings shackled by a life of ease, or as sad and melancholy beasts plaguing the streets inhabited by humans. She listened to the stirrings of that enraged maternal mass, apparently stranded there as if by an accident of fate. A crater seething not with filth and excrement, as might have been expected, but with the rise and fall of living, breathing flesh, long backs and haunches rising and falling, powered by the miracle of oxygen. And so the crust of a scab, a victory over the wound, formed over that entire sector of the city.

Sandra never realized how close she had come to prayer. She had closed her eyes and allowed the odour to enter her. What for, she never asked.

'You should bring your price down', they said. And she found this amusing. They complained. But at first sight of the Zoo's green wall, before Sandra had even opened the door, they already began to tingle with excitement.

The Companions

Mauro Pinheiro

Daniel had already been waiting for over half an hour, seated in a dark lobby. He was still not acclimatized to European temperatures, and used to sweat when it was cold and get goose pimples on the hottest days. He would never get accustomed to it. At this time of day, he could have been on a beach in Luanda, shirtless in the sun, without either sweating or getting gooseflesh; but his destiny had taken a different turn, and now he was here, in the lobby of a stuffy apartment on Lisbon's Campo de Ourique.

The door opened and a man of medium height, wearing a dark square-cut three-piece suit, looked across at him. In one hand he was holding a rolled umbrella and in the other, a white felt hat. His shirt collar was held in place with a bow tie.

'Who are you?' he asked.

Daniel rose to his feet and nodded circumspectly.

'My name is Daniel. I am here to accompany you.'

'Wasn't there someone white available to accompany me?'

'Well... I am not sure. I could leave, if you prefer.'

'Don't be silly. Seeing that you're already here.'

Daniel decided that his need for money came before questions about the colour of his skin. So he gave a dry swallow and slowly descended the staircase, following the ill-tempered creature who rejected accepting his arm in support.

As they stepped out onto the pavement, the man stopped suddenly, looking about him with a perplexed air. Daniel noticed his thin shrunken lips, above which a bushy moustache hovered.

The sun was setting over the seven hills of the city as the two men set out in the direction of the Jardim da Estrela. Daniel thought the old man might wish to sit down on a bench, but he paused only to light a cigarette which paradoxically seemed to give his legs renewed vigour.

'And which colony do you come from?' inquired the old man.

'I'm from Angola. We are no longer a colony but a country.'

'That is simply a matter of one's point of view. I lived a long time in Africa. I don't remember having seen as many blacks as all that over there. So what are so many of them, you included, doing over here?'

Daniel once again felt a pain in his chest, the like of which he'd never known before setting out across the world. He considered protesting, but preferred to pause for a moment to recover his breath and his patience. Then he replied:

'I came over some years ago. And it was already like this.'

The old man resumed his walk. He seemed not to have heard Daniel's reply. It was hardly worth repeating it now: they were entering a busy avenue where cars were hooting and emitting fumes onto the asphalt.

'Ah, Álvaro! Was this the chaos you praised in your odes?'

Daniel concluded he was accompanying a man who was on the brink of losing his faculties. After crossing the road, the old man stopped to light another cigarette. He appeared lost in thought. The matchstick went out before his fingers flicked it away.

When they reached the Miradouro de Santa Catarina, the golden halo of the setting sun was bathing the city below, the shadows outlining the contours of the houses. The waters of the River Tagus reflected the day's last sighs on its silver shield. The old man sat himself down beside him and placed a gaunt and pallid hand on his leg.

> I am the escaped one,
> After I was born
> They locked me up inside me
> But I left.
> My soul seeks me,
> Through hills and valley,
> I hope my soul
> Never finds me.

'What's that?' Daniel asked, startled.

'A little poem from my youth that I composed in English.'

'You're a poet?'

'You can see for yourself it's not too bad. And you, what do you do?'

'Me? I accompany people.'

'Then the two of us have very similar occupations.'

For the first time, Daniel saw him smile. And he smiled too.

Then they were descending the sinuous little alleys leading to the river bank. They walked unhurriedly, observing the banal intimacies of everyday life. A continuous breeze swept along the pavements. Daniel felt neither hot nor cold. A discreet melody was issuing from an upper storey. Washing danced on a line strung between two windows.

'Where are we going?' asked Daniel.

'We've arrived.'

At that instant, a car resembling a Salmson convertible pulled up against the pavement. Daniel was surprised at the appearance—and the clothes—of the four men who jumped out of the vehicle. They seemed affable types. They smiled like friends who hadn't met up in ages.

'Daniel,' said the old man, lighting still another cigarette. 'You may go now. I shall be in the good company of Álvaro, Alberto, Bernardo and Ricardo.'

Then they all got into the car, waved rapidly from the side windows, and set off down the Ribeira das Naus avenue. Daniel looked up and saw the morning star alone in the cobalt sky. At that precise moment, a torrential tempest was unleashed on the white beaches of Luanda.

Kizombar

Kalaf Angelo

On the very last day of 2007, I put up a post on my blog, reflecting on the paths taken by the music movement I belong to. Nothing too special. Just that, having been to a concert performed by one of my mates and since the year was about to end, I was tempted to write a few words on the subject. I wrote a short post on what had been happening in Portugal in relation to urban culture over the last 8 years; it was on the concept of cultural identity we had come to embrace and the need to find a voice, an image that could relay the Euro-African clash that is life in Lisbon to the world, this Luso-Whatever now so familiar and at the same time so strange to us.

I had only recently started keeping a blog, with just 32 posts to date, just one of which elicited a relevant comment. André Chedas, a Portuguese guy who'd gone to live in Barcelona, and who now wanted to return to Lisbon and apply his knowledge of cultural business management to generate a more creative flow within the lusophone world. Defending the affirmation of Lisbon's identity through what he calls 'lusophone cultural fusion', he believes that we now seem further than ever away from seeing coming generation reclaim the joy of Angolan dances such as the *semba*, with its vital, agile, choreography, or to see our friends and family members dancing *kuduro* and *mornas* quite as beautifully as their grandmother sings fados.

I read André's words with a smile and set off to try out a new Japanese restaurant recently opened near to my house. On crossing the Rua dos Fanqueiros I came across a group of friends with nothing particular in mind for a Saturday night. So we all decided to go as far as the Cathedral together, and dine at the said Japanese restaurant. After sushi, we went up from Chiado to the Bairro Alto, which lived up to its High Barrio name. We took a turn around the Rua da Barroca and the Rua da Bica.* Our talk was lively as the music was light and loose, encircling and enfolding us. We weren't dancing, but our movements were almost a dance, and consisted in tapping out the rhythm

---

* Known as 'the most photographed street in Lisbon', it is among the most historic, and contains both the oldest wooden trams and the elevator going from the old town along the river up to the 'Bairro Alto'.

with our feet and unleashing our bodies whenever we recognized a tune.

At around 3 a.m., the Barrio turned down the sounds
and everyone dispersed. The choices lay between going to
Santa Apolónia or Cais do Sodré to take a train. But then
someone in the group suggested one final nightcap before
saying goodbye. We entered a bar where they were talking
Creole and we could hear the sounds of kizomba.* Instantly,
I smelt the scent of the Cape Verdean sea rise all along the
Rua Bica. As soon as we were inside, we literally took possession of the space. All the others there with me were not
only used to the kind of music we were hearing, but also
used to dancing to it. But they weren't African. They were
all about 30 years old and had come into contact with
kizomba during their secondary school years, on forays
out, or to festivals, like Andanças.† Right there before my
eyes, spontaneously and without any plan or preparation or
invocation of romantic Africanism, in the minute space of
a bar the images described by André came to life. It was just
a Saturday like any other in the Lisbon of today.

* An endlessly fluid dance, danced in pairs (like ballroom dancers) and with
some steps similar to the tango. It has its roots in Angola, but is danced also in
Europe and Latin America. *Kizombar*, the title of this story, means 'to dance—or
move to—the Kizomba'.

† The international festival of popular dance held annually in Portugal. It
includes 'fusions'—contemporary adaptations of earlier dances from many lusophone regions—including those described here.

A Time When

Kalaf Angelo

I wouldn't precisely say that the time actually passed quickly. Lisbon is a city which lends itself to going slow and, if we weren't in a hurry, it would be the ideal space in which to ramble on about the natural disorder of just about anything in the universe. The heat makes us breathe heavily, overheated and red-cheeked, our heartbeats irregular, to the point where gradually everything becomes an effort, where the only attractive prospect is of stretching out our limbs on some street corner, staying put as if every day were one long Sunday.

I arrived with a suitcase in one hand and a fistful of dreams in the other. The dream of return remained overwhelmingly present. But from the very first moment music made itself felt and Lisbon, with its infectious indolence, invited me to stay. From that moment on it became more than a city, it became my city, my country. That was 14 years ago. At that time, DJVibe still went by the name of Tó Pereira, and hip-hop had not got beyond being a joke— mere small morsels from the edge, with its rhymes, its slang manufactured in the USA, creating art from the lack of self-esteem and the dominant nothingness. The rest got lost among the dust clouds of the intersecting ways at Marqués de Pombal.*

The following years were devoted to exploring each of Lisbon's seven hills in turn. We were trying to reach and understand the source of every musical current, however significant or not, from Bairro Alto to 24 de Julho, Santa Apolónia to Docas. We started with Heróis do Mar,† our proud lusophones, shouting out the refrain: 'Yo! He can't swim!', leading into the rise of Geração Rasca,‡ of long

* A major central square containing little but traffic and the Rococo statue of the Marques in the middle.

† Heróis do Mar was a Portuguese pop rock band formed in March 1981. The group disbanded in 1990. Their name is taken from the first line of the Portuguese national anthem: 'Heróis do mar, nobre povo' (Heroes of the sea, noble people...). The last line of the chorus, 'Contra os canhões marchar, marchar!' (Against the cannons, march, march!), is an alteration of the original, 'Contra os bretões marchar, marchar' (Against the Britons, march, march!), a call to arms against the 1890 British Ultimatum.

‡ On 23 March 2011, Prime Minister José Sócrates resigned when new austerity measures failed a Parliamentary vote. Geração à Rasca (Scratch Generation) was formed, a protest movement in which musicians and other activists were prominent, committed to 'Make every citizen a politician', a slogan from José Saramago's Nobel Prize-winning acceptance speech.

nights with the battle cries of the band echoing through the streets of the neighbourhood, followed by mornings spent visiting the thieves' flea market, in search of rare vinyl and second-hand clothes, in the name of a style to be worn with all the skill of young models parading in the annual *Manobras de Maio* self-styled fashion parades.

There is a pleasure in looking back to Lisbon yesterday in the attempt to understand it today. Who its inhabitants are, their comings and goings, how they live and how they beat the luso-blues. Many of their experiences appear in Edgar Pera's films or Da Weasel's songs, the best of which date from the time when Yen Sung was Master of Ceremonies, with DJ Johnny spinning the discs at the gateway to the track up to Três Pastorinhos,* affording the perfect soundtrack to discovering Lisbon. It all dates back to the period when the closest thing to a playlist on an iPod was a collection of tape cassettes, which had to be categorized according to musical type, or to geography and passions either consummated or left unconsummated. All this was long before Oxigénio or Radar. Without all this, what would have become of our immense minority?

At the time President Cavaco Silva was in power, the European Union reigned and the country seemed to be progressing. Nowadays we are starting to ask questions

* In 1917, the three 'little shepherds' (aged between 7 and 10 years old), now canonized by the Catholic Church, saw visions of the Virgin Mary and of an Angel of Peace on this track leading to Fatima.

about this progress... I am not looking for answers, although this may be a subject for another chronicle. First of all, I would prefer to look back to the days when the shanty-town of Casal Ventoso was one vast supermarket selling wraps of highspeed dreams, and where I witnessed so much talented youth embark on a one-way trip.*

Going slowly, we let ourselves ramble on about the natural disorder in the things of our world, tracing improbable routes from Marvila to Linhas, Campo Grande to the main square of Rossio, from the tram 28 terminus to the bar with the best salt cod, from sunset by the river to Zé's nights of Guinea-Bissau be-bop.

* Portugal decriminalized the use of all drugs in 2001.

Notes on the Authors

Eça de Queiroz (Póvoa de Varzim, north Portugal, 25 November 1845–Paris, 16 August 1900) Arguably the most celebrated Realist novelist in the Portuguese canon, Eça de Queiroz has been hailed as the equal of Dickens, Proust, and Tolstoy, less than half of his novels being published during his lifetime (excluding Alves & Cia). Born to an unmarried teenager (his father only recognized him when Eça de Queiroz was forty), he attended Coimbra University before entering the diplomatic service, serving as consul in Havana, Newcastle, Bristol, and Paris. He wrote approximately 30 novels, novellas, and extended short stories, including The Crime of Father Amaro (1875), Cousin Bazilio (1878), The Mandarin (1880), and The Maias (1880); and left behind him a trunk containing a mass of unpublished manuscripts, including Alves & Ca., essentially a comic satire. There have been at least three recent and different translations of this novel into English.

Fernando Pessoa (Lisbon, 13 June 1888–Lisbon, 30 November 1935) Portuguese poet, writer, literary critic, translator, publisher, and philosopher, Pessoa is described as one of the most significant literary figures of the twentieth century and one of the greatest poets in the Portuguese language.

Raised, from the age of six, in Durban he was an anglophile who also wrote in English, sometimes in French. Pessoa was a prolific writer, employing over eighty authorial voices. He called them *heteronyms* rather than 'pseudonyms', capturing and naming each independent intellectual voice. Among his most famous works is *The Book of Disquiet*, which has at least four recent English translations. However, in his lifetime, Pessoa published just four poetry collections in English and one in Portuguese (*Mensagem*, 1933). He left a mass of unpublished, often unfinished manuscripts, housed in the Nati,onal Library since 1988. *A Estrada do Esquecimento* contains a recent prose selection, mostly untranslated.

Soeiro Pereira Gomes (Baião, 14 April 1909–Lisbon, 5 December 1949) Together with Alves Redol, Fernando Namora, and Manuel da Fonseca, Gomes is an initiator of the movement known as Portuguese Neo-Realism and a major name in twentieth-century Portuguese literature. His writing was integral to his militancy in the Portuguese Communist Party. Although banned by Portugal's Prime Minister António de Oliveira Salazar, Gomes was a member of its Central Committee, and its Lisbon headquarters are named after him. He began writing journalism (for *O Diabo*) by the age of twenty and is primarily known for two major novels (*Esteiros* and *Engrenagem*). The work is steeped both in socialist realism and in his experience as a manual labourer in agriculture and industry. Like the character in 'Lost Refuge', he was forced to operate underground under Salazar's dictatorship. This clandestine existence prevented him from seeking medical attention when he developed lung cancer and he died aged only forty.

José Rodrigues Miguéis (Lisbon, 9 December 1901–New York, 27 October 1980) Born in Lisbon with a Galician father, who raised him with progressive and Republican views, Miguéis studied law, for which he decided he had little talent. He added a further degree in literature and pedagogy at Brussels, qualifying as a teacher in 1933. In 1935, he emigrated to the United States, obtaining citizenship in 1942. There he worked as a teacher and as translator and editor for numerous magazines, including *Reader's Digest*. Although he never returned to live in Portugal for more than short periods, he wrote two dozen novels in Portuguese and received both the Prémio Casa da Imprensa (1932) and the Ordem Militar de Santiago da Espada (1979). It is typical of his politics that his 'magnum opus' should have the title *Idealista no mundo real* (Idealist in the Real World). His work is translated into over a dozen languages.

Mário Dionísio (Lisbon, 16 July 1916–Lisbon, 17 November 1993) Dionísio qualified in philology at Lisbon University in 1940, and became a school teacher and then, following the 'Carnation Revolution', university lecturer in Lisbon. He was multitalented across numerous disciplines, an artist and critic as well as an author. He wrote a number of works on fine art, including the biography *Vincent Van Gogh* (1947) and the five-volume *A Paleta e o Mundo* (1956). He was also a prolific arts journalist and music critic, and won major national prizes for his *Essays* (1963) and *Cultural Features* (1964), as well as the Literary Critics' Award (1981) and the *Prémio Atena* (1989). In addition to his fiction, his published works include numerous volumes of poetry, short stories, and an autobiography. In 2009, a cultural institute, named the Centro Mário Dionísio, was opened in Lisbon.

Agustina Bessa-Luís (Vila Meã, Amarante, 15 November 1922–)
Agustina Bessa-Luís is a Portuguese novelist, short story writer,
playwright, and essayist, born in the north of Portugal, near
Amarante. She has won numerous prizes, including both the
Prémio Camões and the Premio Virgílio Ferreira in 2004.
She has written over forty novels, a number of which were
adapted for the cinema by the late great Portuguese filmmaker
Manoel de Oliveira. Much of Bessa-Luís's writing focuses
on the inner lives and intimate conflicts of women, their
attachment to mysticism and the sublime, and their sense
of alienation in relation to the dominant masculine culture.
In fact, her celebrated 1954 novel, *A Sibila* (The Sybil), is often
seen as a watershed for twentieth-century women's writing
in Portugal. Bessa-Luís retired from writing in 2006 for health
reasons.

José Saramago (Azinhaga, 16 November 1922–Lanzarote,
Spain, 18 June 2010) Saramago, first a campaigning journalist, then a novelist, straddled both popular and high culture.
Over two million of his books have been sold in Portugal
and have been translated into 25 languages. Saramago,
awarded the Nobel Prize for Literature in 1998, was a found-
ing member of the National Front for the Defense of Culture
in Lisbon in 1992 and, with Orhan Pamuk, of the European
Writers' Parliament. A militant if libertarian Communist,
Saramago parodied institutions such as the Catholic Church,
the European Union, and the International Monetary Fund.
Following political censorship of his novel The Gospel
According to Jesus Christ in 1992, Saramago went into
exile on Lanzarote, living there until his death. Journey to
Portugal describes his first return to his home country after
his years of exile, reviewing it anew. One novel, *The Year of*

the Death of Ricardo Reis (1984), is also a homage named after one of Pessoa's most famous heteronyms.

Orlanda Amarílis (Assomada, Sta. Catarina, Cape Verde, 8 October 1924–1 February 2014) Orlanda Amarílis Lopes Rodrigues Fernandes Ferreira, known simply as Orlanda Amarílis, was a Cape Verdean writer born into a family of distinguished literary figures, including the poet Baltazar Lopes da Silva and her father, Armando Napoleão Rodrigues Fernandes, who published Cabo Verde's first Creole–Portuguese dictionary. Together with her husband, the writer Manuel Ferriera, Amarílis, she travelled widely, promoting her literature and taking part in cultural interventions in countries as far flung as Angola, Canada, Egypt, Spain, the USA, Goa, Mozambique, Nigeria, and Sudan. She was a member of a number of political organizations including the Portuguese Movement Against Apartheid and The Portuguese Peace Movement. Particularly significant as a writer of short stories, Amarílis' main themes revolved around portrayals of Cape Verdean women and depictions of emigrants of the Cape Verdean diaspora. Both themes are in evidence in *Cais do Sodré Té Salamansa* (Cais do Sodré to Salamansa), a collection published in 1974 and regarded as her masterpiece.

Teolinda Gersão (Coimbra, 30 January 1940–) Gersão studied at the universities of Coimbra, Tübingen, and Berlin. She also taught at the Technical University of Berlin, Lisbon University, and the Universidade Nova de Lisboa, among others, and has been a writer-in-residence at Berkeley, California. A full-time writer since the mid-1990s, Gersão is the author of some twenty novels, several set in Mozambique or Brazil, where she lived for two years. Her early novel *The Word Tree* has been translated into English by Margaret Jull Costa. Her work has received some of the most important awards for novels and short stories in Portugal and four of her books were adapted for the theatre and staged in Portugal, Germany, and Romania. Two short-stories inspired short films and a film based on the novel *Passages* is currently being made. Her books have been translated into eleven languages.

Mário de Carvalho (Lisbon, 25 September 1944–) Mário Costa Martins de Carvalho is a novelist, short story writer, playwright, and screenwriter. During the Portuguese dictatorship, he was arrested by the PIDE, Prime Minister António de Oliveira Salazar's secret police, consequently becoming a staunch opponent of the regime. Having spent fourteen months as a political prisoner, he escaped to Lund, Sweden, where he claimed political asylum shortly before the Carnation Revolution that would bring about Portuguese democracy. His breakthrough as a writer came in 1981 with a collection of short stories entitled *Contos da Sétima Esfera* (Tales from the Seventh Sphere). In 1994, he published the novel *A God Strolling in the Cool of the Evening*, which won various awards and was translated into numerous languages, including into English by Gregory Rabassa, translator of Gabriel García Márquez's *One Hundred Years of Solitude*. Critics have often commented on the versatility and originality of his writing, and the sense of humour which has remained a constant throughout his experiments with genre.

Hélia Correia (Lisbon, February 1949–) Hélia Correia was born in Lisbon and raised in her mother's home town of Mafra. She is a novelist, playwright, poet, and translator and was awarded Portugal's most prestigious literary prize, the

Prémio Camões, for her short story collection *20 Degraus e Ourtos Contos* (Twenty Steps and Other Tales) in 2015. Correia began publishing poetry in literary supplements and magazines in 1968 when she was only nineteen. Her debut as a novelist came in 1981 with *O Separar das Águas* (The Parting of the Waters), and her books proceeded to earn both critical acclaim and commercial success. Her writing is often considered to be inspired by myth, and she has reinterpreted a number of the Greek myths containing female heroines for the stage, including those of Medea, Antigone, and Helen of Troy. Correia also writes for children, and has translated and adapted versions of Shakespeare's *The Tempest* and *A Midsummer Night's Dream* to be performed by young people.

Mauro Pinheiro (Río de Janeiro, 6 January 1957–) Mauro Pinheiro is a writer and translator. Four of his novels (*Cemitério de navios* (1993), *Concerto para corda e pescoço* (2000), *Quando só restar o mundo* (2002), *Estranhos animais* (2007)) and two collections of short stories (*Aquidauana* (1997), *Os caminhantes* (2008)) have been published in Brazil, his country of origin. *Aquidauana* won the National Library of Brazil's Best Reading Award. Pinheiro has translated over a hundred books of literature, philosophy, and history from English or French into Portuguese. They include *Germinal* by Emile Zola (2012), *1973* by Victor Hugo (2017), *Promesse de l'Aube* by Romain Gary (2008), *Canada* by Richard Ford (2016), and *Asta's Book* by Ruth Rendell (2001). He now lives in Arles, France.

Kalaf Angelo Epalanga (Benguela, Angola, 1978–) Kalaf Epalanga is a musician and writer born in Benguela, Angola, and has been living in Lisbon since the 1990s. He is one of the founders of the MTV Europe Award-winning band

Buraka Som Sistema, and the record label *A Enchufada*, which defines itself as 'eradicating musical borders since 2006'. He has also written literary chronicles for one of Portugal's most prestigious newspapers, *O Público*, a selection of which were collected under the title *Estórias de Amor Para Meninos de Cor* (Love Stories for Children of Colour) using his stage name, Kalaf Angelo. Epalanga published his first novel, *Também os Brancos Sabem Dançar* (White People Also Know How to Dance), in 2017.

Further Reading

The First Global Village: How Portugal Changed the World, Martin Page, Casa das Letras, 2002.

Wrath of God: The Great Lisbon Earthquake of 1755, Edward Paice, Quercus, 2009.

Lisbon: War in the Shadow of the City of Light, 1939–1945, Neill Lochery, Public Affairs 2012.

Conquerors: How Portugal Seized the Indian Ocean and Forged the First Global Empire, Roger Crowley, Faber and Faber, 2015.

Take Six: Six Portuguese Women Writers, Margaret Jull Costa (Ed.), Dedalus Ltd., 2018.

The Last Kabbalist of Lisbon, Richard Zimler, Corsair, 2014.

Pereira Maintains, Antonio Tabucchi (Patrick Creagh trans.), Canons, 2015.

The Return, Dulce Maria Cardoso (Angel Gurria-Quintana trans.), MacLehose Press, 2017.

Night Train to Lisbon, Pascal Mercier, Atlantic Books, 2009.

A Small Death in Lisbon, Robert Wilson, Harper Collins, 2009.

The Year of the Death of Ricardo Reis, José Saramago (Giovanni Pontiero trans.), Harvill, 1998.

Baltasar and Blimunda, José Saramago (Giovanni Pontiero trans.), Vintage Classics, 2001.

The Book of Disquiet, Fernando Pessoa (Margaret Jull Costa trans.), Penguin Modern Classics, 2015.

The Night in Lisbon, Erich Maria Remarque (Ralph Manheim trans.), Ballantine Books, 1998.

The Piano Cemetery, José Luís Peixoto (Daniel Hahn trans.), Bloomsbury, 2010.

Echowave, Joe Joyce, New Island Books, 2017.

A Little Larger Than the Entire Universe: Selected Poems, Fernando Pessoa (Richard Zenith trans.), Penguin Classics, 2006.

Publisher's Acknowledgements

Eça de Queiroz, *Alves & Companhia*, pp. 30–8. Chardron, 1880/1925.

Fernando Pessoa, *A Estrada do Esquecimento e outros contos*, pp. 43–59. Assírio & Alvim, 2015.

Soeiro Pereira Gomes, 'Refúgio Perdido', in *Refúgio Perdido e outros contos*, pp. 34–43. Avante! [PCP], 1975. With the kind permission of *Avante!*

José Rodrigues Miguéis, 'O Acidente', from *Onde a Noite se Acaba*, pp. 197–217. Editorial Estúdios Cor, 1968. With the kind permission of Monica Teresa Miguéis Jakobs.

Mário Dionisio, 'Assobiando à Vontade', from *O Dia Cinzento*, pp. 85–96. Coimbra Editora, 1944. With the kind permission of Eduarda Dionísio.

Agustina Bessa-Luís, 'O Noivo', from *Contos Impopulares*, pp. 105–12. Guimarães and Co, 1953/1984. © Agustina Bessa-Luís, in 'Contos impopulares', 1953. By arrangement with Literarische Agentur Mertin Inh. Nicole Witt e. K., Frankfurt am Main, Germany, and with the kind permission of Mónica Baldaque.

José Saramago, 'They Say It's a Good Thing', from *Journey to Portugal*, trans. Amanda Hopkinson and Nick Caistor, pp. 328–48. Harvill Press/Random House, 1990/2000.

For permission to publish in the USA, Canada, and Open Market: 'They Say it's a Good Thing' from *Journey to Portugal* by José Saramago, translated from the Portuguese by Amanda Hopkinson and Nick Caistor. Copyright © 1990 by José Saramago. English translation copyright © 2000 by Amanda Hopkinson and Nick Caistor. Reprinted by permission of Houghton Mifflin Harcourt Publishing Company. All rights reserved.

For permission to publish in the UK and Commonwealth and Europe: from *Journey to Portugal* by José Saramago, translated by Amanda Hopkinson and Nick Caistor. Published by The Harvill Press. Reprinted by permission of The Random House Group Limited © 2000.

Orlanda Amarílis, 'Cais do Sodré', from *Cais-do-Sodré té Salamansa*, pp. 8–21. Centelha, 1974. With the kind permission of Hernâni Donaldo Napoleão Ferreira.

Teolinda Gersão, 'Natureza Morta Com Cabeça de Goraz', from *Histórias de Ver e Andar*, pp. 148–57. Dom Quixote, 2002. With the kind permission of Teolinda Gersão.

Mário de Carvalho, 'Coleccionadores', from *Contos da Sétime Esfera*, pp. 187–97. Caminho, 2010. © Mário de Carvalho, in 'Contos da sétima esfera', 1981. By arrangement with Literarische Agentur Mertin Inh. Nicole Witt e. K., Frankfurt am Main, Germany.

Hélia Correia, 'Metro Zoo', from *Vinte Degraus e outros contos*, pp. 31–6. Relógio d'Água, 2014. With the kind permission of Hélia Correia. By arrangement with the Sociedade Portuguesa de Autores.

Mauro Pinheiro, 'The Companions'. With the kind permission of Mauro Pinheiro.

Kalaf Angelo (Epalanga), 'Kizombar' and 'No Tempo em Que', from *Estórias de Amor Para Meninos de Cor*, pp. 12–14, 69–71. Caminho, 2011. © Kalaf Epalanga, in "Estórias de Amor para

Meninos de Cor", 2011. By arrangement with Literarische Agentur Mertin Inh. Nicole Witt e. K., Frankfurt am Main, Germany.

Every attempt has been made to contact copyright holders for permission to publish. Anyone wishing to assert their rights with regard to the contents of this anthology should contact OUP.

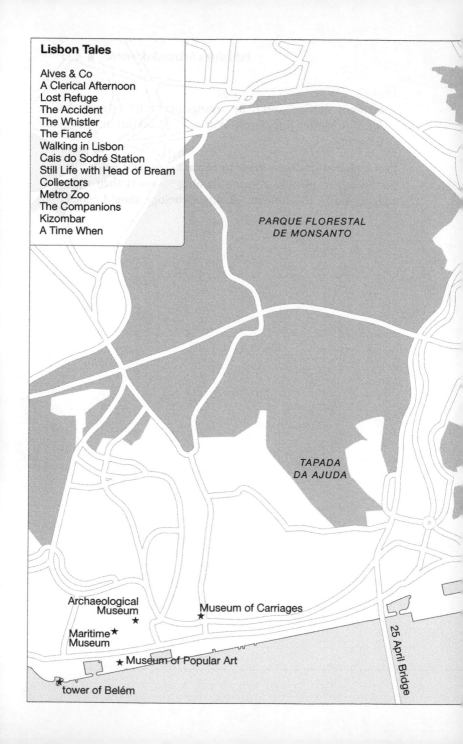

Lisbon Tales

Alves & Co
A Clerical Afternoon
Lost Refuge
The Accident
The Whistler
The Fiancé
Walking in Lisbon
Cais do Sodré Station
Still Life with Head of Bream
Collectors
Metro Zoo
The Companions
Kizombar
A Time When

*PARQUE FLORESTAL
DE MONSANTO*

*TAPADA
DA AJUDA*

Archaeological
Museum ★

Museum of Carriages ★

Maritime ★
Museum

★ Museum of Popular Art

★ tower of Belém

25 April Bridge

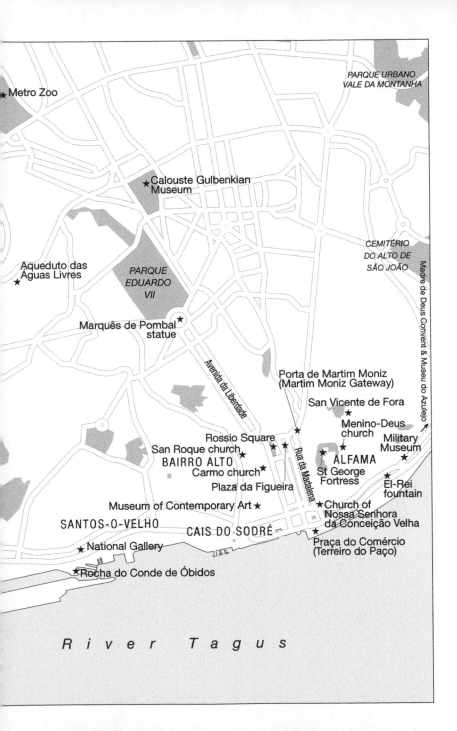